The Watcher's Silent Crusade : A Police Procedurals & Crime Thriller

Marcelo Palacios

Published by INDEPENDENT PUBLISHER, 2024.

This is a work of fiction. Similarities to real people, places, or events are entirely coincidental.

THE WATCHER'S SILENT CRUSADE : A POLICE PROCEDURALS & CRIME THRILLER

First edition. November 20, 2024.

Copyright © 2024 Marcelo Palacios.

ISBN: 979-8230533726

Written by Marcelo Palacios.

Also by Marcelo Palacios

El Club de los Pecados Un Thriller Psicológico
La Habitación Resonante Un Thriller Psicológico
Mentiras en Código Un Thriller Político
The Political Lies A Political Thriller
Sin's Fraternity A Psychological Thriller
El Cuarto de los Ecos Un Thriller Psicologico lleno de Suspenso
The Room of Echoes A Psychological Thriller Full of Suspense
El Espejo Perturbador Un Thriller Psicologico
The Disturbing Mirror A Psychological Thriller
Luces Apagadas en la Ciudad Brillante Un Thriller Psicológico,Crimen y Policial
Lights Out in the Shining City A Psychological, Crime and Police Thriller
Under the Cloak of Horror A Criminal Psychological Thriller full of Abuse, Corruption, Mystery, Suspense and Adventure
The Housemaid's Shadow A Psychological Thriller
Unraveling Marriage, Unraveling Divorce A Domestic Thriller
Mindstorm Protocol Expansion : A Post-Apocalyptic, Dystopian and Technological Thriller Science Fiction Novel
The Power of Invisible Chains : A Conspiracy, Crime & Political Thriller
The Watcher's Silent Crusade : A Police Procedurals & Crime Thriller
Very Bad Momentum : A Short Story

Table of Contents

Chapter 1: The First Strike 1
Chapter 2: The Clue in the Shadows 5
Chapter 3: Whispers of Corruption 9
Chapter 4: A Cold Trail 13
Chapter 5: The Forensic Truth 17
Chapter 6: The Spectator's Message 20
Chapter 7: Tangled Webs 24
Chapter 8: The Journalist's Perspective 28
Chapter 9: A Target in Plain Sight 32
Chapter 10: The Digital Footprint 35
Chapter 11: Uncovering the Past 38
Chapter 12: The Informant's Call 41
Chapter 13: The Hunter Becomes the Hunted 44
Chapter 14: The Meeting in the Shadows 47
Chapter 15: The Witness Who Knows Too Much 51
Chapter 16: The Silent Crusade 55
Chapter 17: The Deal with the Devil 58
Chapter 18: The Web of Lies 61
Chapter 19: The Shadow of Betrayal 64
Chapter 20: The Pursuit of Justice 68
Chapter 21: The Last Clue 71
Chapter 22: Into the Lion's Den 74
Chapter 23: The Face Behind the Mask 78
Chapter 24: The Price of Truth 82
Chapter 25: The Price of Redemption 86
Chapter 26: The Deadly Game 89
Chapter 27: The Haunting Truth 92
Chapter 28: The Final Confrontation 95
Chapter 29: Aftermath and Reflection 99
Chapter 30: The Weight of Betrayal 102
Chapter 31: The Final Revelation 105
Chapter 32: The Shadow in the Ranks 109
Chapter 33: A Final Confrontation 113

Chapter 34: The Unbreakable Oath 117

Chapter 1: The First Strike

City lights blinked in and out through a hazy mist as the rain began to pour, a steady rhythm of drops hitting the cracked asphalt. Patrol cars lined the street, casting red and blue strobes across the old stone building towering over the scene. Yellow tape sliced through the crowd, a feeble barrier against the onlookers craning for a better look. Some faces glowed with sick curiosity, others murmured questions to each other, voices tense.

I ducked under the tape, the weight of my badge pulling heavy at my side. Officers turned, gave me space, their voices cutting off mid-sentence. The call had come in just past midnight: a body, some politician. High-profile, with connections wound thick as vines through City Hall's core. It didn't take much to feel the tension rippling through the air. This was no random killing, no unlucky mugging.

I moved past the line of officers, giving a brief nod to my mentor, Inspector Jacob Thorne, standing just outside the building's entrance. His face was carved from granite, eyes fixed on the doorway like he was bracing himself for what lay beyond. The media would descend on this scene by morning, and any mistake would amplify tenfold. He caught my eye and nodded, a flicker of something unreadable in his gaze.

Inside, the stench hit hard. A metallic tang sharpened by the blood smeared across the marble floors. The old architecture only seemed to trap the smell, heavy as the smoke-stained curtains clinging to the walls. I found the victim sprawled near the base of the grand staircase, a crimson mess against the polished stone.

Councilman Marcus Langston. Late fifties. A man who had once filled television screens with speeches promising a "new era" for the city. The gray hair and deep creases lining his face looked worn even in death. The meticulous precision of the wounds was striking—an almost surgical savagery. A clean, deep slash to the carotid, another to the chest. No signs of a struggle, no misplaced fury. Just clinical and calculated.

Dr. Liam Byrne, the forensic analyst, knelt by the body, taking measurements and making careful notes. He looked up as I approached, his gloved hands moving to adjust his glasses. "It's... precise. Whoever did this didn't waste any effort. They knew exactly where to cut and how deep."

I crouched, examining the lines of blood seeping into the cracks between the stones. "One blow to the neck, then the heart. Quick, efficient. Military, maybe."

Byrne shook his head, holding up a small evidence bag. Inside, a slip of paper. Typed words, just a few lines, but enough to make the hair at the back of my neck prickle. "The Spectator has spoken," it read.

No fingerprints, no smudges. The words gleamed black against the white paper, chilling in their simplicity.

I turned to Byrne, eyebrow raised. "The Spectator?"

He shrugged, his lips pressed into a thin line. "First time I've seen anything like it. No hits in the database under that name. Whoever this is, they're either very new, or very, very careful."

I rose, scanning the perimeter, feeling the weight of the silent message hanging in the air. The officers stood back, watching with that uneasy respect that only surfaced at scenes like this. One of them, a rookie, was pale, his gaze fixed on the bloody letters smeared just above the councilman's head. Byrne hadn't noticed them yet, but I knew what they said.

"The City Will Fall."

Words bold, written with confidence. Someone had scrawled them just above Langston's body, angled in a way meant to be seen immediately. This wasn't just murder. This was a declaration.

Thorne entered, his gaze sharp and sweeping over the scene. He moved like a storm contained, glancing at the bloodied letters and the message in the evidence bag. His jaw tightened as he turned to me.

"Whoever they are, they wanted this found. They wanted us to know exactly who's in control," he said, voice a low murmur.

I nodded, still studying the letters. The precision of the killing, the starkness of the message—it was an artful display of power, crafted to invoke fear. A statement that wouldn't go ignored.

Thorne turned his gaze back to the scene, his voice edged with something almost like admiration. "This wasn't random. The Spectator wanted Langston dead for a reason, and they want the city to see it. This is the kind of message you only send when you're just getting started."

The rookie officer from before shifted uncomfortably, his gaze darting to the crimson letters and back to us. His face was ashen, and he swallowed hard, as if trying to gather the courage to speak. "Detective, Inspector... Do you think they'll strike again?"

The question hung in the air, too heavy for an easy answer. I glanced at Thorne, who gave a curt nod, signaling I should take this one.

"We're dealing with someone who sees the city as their playground," I said, voice firm. "They didn't just want Langston dead. They wanted the impact, the fear, and the attention. That kind of person... they rarely stop at one."

The rookie nodded, swallowing again, then backed away, his face ghostly pale as he melted back into the ranks of officers.

I turned to Byrne, motioning to the paper in the evidence bag. "Get this analyzed. I want every detail. If there's even a hint of a fingerprint or trace, I want to know."

Byrne gave a sharp nod, tucking the bag carefully into his kit. "On it. I'll have preliminary results by morning."

The councilman's face stared up at us, frozen in that eternal mask of death. The lights overhead cast harsh shadows across his features, making him look almost statuesque, a reminder of what power once held—and how easily it could be taken.

Thorne moved closer, his hand resting briefly on my shoulder. "Emma, we're going to need a list of his associates, any enemies. Someone didn't just kill Langston. They killed a piece of this city."

I nodded, already mentally sifting through the councilman's known connections, his allies, his opponents. Langston was the kind of man who left strong impressions, both good and bad. Somewhere among them, we'd find the link. A spark of motive, a connection that tied him to the Spectator.

"Everyone in this room has a role," I said quietly, meeting Thorne's gaze. "Langston was just the beginning. Whatever they're planning, they're targeting something big. It's not just about individuals—it's about the city."

A heavy silence followed my words, the weight of it pressing against us all. The first strike had been delivered, a brutal, calculated blow meant to shake the city's foundations. And judging by the killer's chilling message, this was only the start.

Thorne and I exchanged a final look, the unspoken understanding between us. We were on borrowed time, racing against a shadow we couldn't yet see. But I'd find the Spectator, no matter the cost. I'd unravel their game, piece by twisted piece, and bring them into the light.

Chapter 2: The Clue in the Shadows

Thorne's flashlight beam swept across the wall, lingering on the jagged letters smeared in blood just above the victim's head. "The City Will Fall." The words felt heavier now, more menacing in the grim silence of the early morning hours, and for a moment, Thorne and I stood side by side, staring at the message left by the killer. The press and the public would be swarming City Hall by daylight. We had to work fast.

"We're dealing with a methodical mind," Thorne murmured, his voice barely louder than a whisper. "This isn't some maniac. This is someone who knows what they're doing and why."

I ran my fingers along the wall beside the letters, feeling for anything—a hidden indentation, a smear the killer might have left behind. The ink-black blood glistened under the harsh beam of Thorne's light, and my instincts told me there was more here than we could see. My hands moved lower, hovering over a faint symbol etched in blood just below the message. A small eye, watching, unblinking.

"Did you catch this?" I asked, pointing toward the hidden mark. Thorne leaned in, his face impassive as he examined it.

"An eye," he said, more to himself than to me. "The Spectator, then." He tilted his head, piecing it together in his mind. "They want us to know they're watching, that they've been watching."

The stillness of the room settled around us, punctuated only by the soft shuffling of Byrne, collecting samples nearby. For a killer like the Spectator, this wasn't just a message; it was an invitation. Whoever they were, they felt secure enough to mock us, to challenge us. Thorne straightened, and I could see his jaw tighten, his eyes narrowing as he processed the implications.

"We should review Langston's recent public appearances," I suggested, flipping open my notebook and jotting down everything I could remember from his speeches. "Maybe there's a speech, an event, something that could've painted a target on his back."

Thorne nodded. "And his private life. Langston was no saint." He ran a hand over his chin, looking past me at the crimson letters, then back to the councilman's corpse sprawled on the marble floor. "We need to start with his connections at City Hall. Friends, enemies. If the Spectator is targeting the city's elite, Langston won't be the last."

The city's elite. Politicians, business leaders, public figures—people who believed themselves untouchable, safe behind money and influence. I felt a shiver run through me as I scribbled more notes, trying to anticipate the Spectator's next move. Byrne came up beside us, a sealed bag of blood samples in one hand.

"I've got what I need for now," he said, nodding to the wall. "The blood matches Langston's, but there's something off about the way it's spread. Looks deliberate, almost ritualistic."

Thorne grunted, folding his arms across his chest. "That's because it is. The Spectator isn't just trying to kill—this is about something bigger."

The thought hung in the air between us. A political message in blood. The more I thought about it, the more I realized just how calculated it was. Langston, after all, had been a fixture of City Hall. If there was anyone in this city who would draw attention, it was him.

I walked back over to the message, kneeling in front of the councilman's body, studying the angles. The letters slanted ever so slightly to the left, and the eye symbol was centered perfectly below it. A symmetry to the brutality, an intentional pattern. I couldn't shake the feeling that the Spectator wanted us to see the care they'd put into their work.

"Langston had plenty of enemies," I said, voicing my thoughts aloud. "Anyone ambitious enough to run for public office has people who'd want him dead. But why go to this much trouble? Why the message?"

Thorne's eyes darkened, the gears in his mind turning as he examined the letters again. "Maybe the message wasn't just for us, Emma. Maybe it was for others like Langston. The Spectator wants power players to know they're vulnerable, that their status won't protect them."

The idea lingered, twisting uneasily in my gut. "And the eye?" I asked. "Why leave that symbol?"

"It's a signature. A mark of ownership." Thorne's voice was grim. "Our killer wants control over this city. They're not just out to kill; they're out to send a message of fear, to make everyone look over their shoulders, question who might be watching."

Byrne finished bagging the last of the samples and moved back, giving us the space we needed to study the scene without interruption. I knew Byrne's report would help, but I wasn't counting on forensic science alone to solve this. The Spectator was playing a psychological game, using the city's most powerful as pawns. And I had the uncomfortable feeling that we'd only seen the opening move.

Thorne glanced at his watch, then at me. "We need to move on Langston's close contacts," he said. "Politicians, family, business associates—anyone who stood to gain from his death."

I followed Thorne to the door, casting one last look back at the councilman's body. The stillness of it, the deliberate placement, the eye symbol. The Spectator's handiwork seemed almost ritualistic, a warning to the rest of the city that no one was untouchable. As we exited the building, I couldn't shake the feeling that the Spectator was watching us, that somewhere out there, a pair of eyes marked our every move.

Back at the precinct, we gathered around a map of the city, marking key locations tied to Langston's life. Thorne tapped his pen against a few points—City Hall, Langston's estate, the law firm where he'd once practiced.

"We start here." Thorne's voice held a note of finality. "Langston's inner circle. Find out who had the means, who had the motive. And keep in mind—this wasn't a spur-of-the-moment attack. The Spectator has been watching."

He glanced at me, his eyes sharper than I'd ever seen them. "This is the first strike, Emma, but it won't be the last. We're dealing with someone who sees the city as a chessboard. We can't afford to be two moves behind."

The adrenaline buzzed beneath my skin as I took in his words, mentally noting our next steps. We were facing something larger than a single killer. The Spectator was making their presence known, and I knew, without a doubt, that they wouldn't stop with Langston.

As I pored over the files in the dim precinct light, the pieces of Langston's life slowly came into focus. His connections, his deals, his alliances with other city officials. The money that had flowed freely in and out of his accounts. But none of it told me why the Spectator had chosen him as their first victim.

Every lead seemed to fork off in two directions, with no clear path forward. And yet, the eye kept resurfacing, staring back at me from the crime scene photos, as if daring me to solve the puzzle it represented. The more I searched for connections, the more the web tangled, pulling me deeper into the Spectator's game.

I heard Thorne's voice over my shoulder, calm yet urgent. "We're just getting started. But we're not alone in this. The Spectator wants us to follow. They're leaving breadcrumbs, and they're counting on us to find them."

I glanced back at him, meeting his gaze. This killer was no random threat. They were watching us as closely as we watched them, calculating each move with a level of patience I hadn't seen before. The game was on, and every instinct told me we'd need to stay two steps ahead if we were going to survive it.

Chapter 3: Whispers of Corruption

The air in City Hall felt thick with tension. Even the fluorescent lights overhead seemed dimmer, casting long shadows down empty hallways where whispers died out the second Thorne and I approached. I had spent my fair share of time here, but today, the walls held secrets that seemed to seep into every corner, waiting to pounce.

Thorne and I headed to the office of Councilman David Haynes, one of Langston's closest associates. If anyone knew why Langston had been targeted, it would be him. Haynes was younger than most of the officials, with sharp eyes and a habit of choosing his words carefully. As we entered, his gaze drifted toward the closed door, almost as if he feared it would swing open to reveal someone listening.

"What can I do for you, detectives?" Haynes' voice came out smooth, but his hands twisted slightly, betraying his nerves.

I leaned forward, letting the weight of my stare settle on him. "Councilman Langston's murder wasn't random, Councilman. Whoever did this knew exactly who they were targeting. We're trying to piece together who might have had a reason to make him disappear."

Haynes ran a hand over his tie, his eyes flicking between me and Thorne. "Langston... had his fingers in a lot of pies, so to speak. He wasn't shy about pushing boundaries." He paused, choosing his words. "Or making enemies."

Thorne's jaw tightened. "Enemies where? Are we talking personal grudges or something bigger?"

Haynes looked down at his desk, hesitating. "Langston was... ambitious. He was involved in several city projects. Some of those projects benefitted certain individuals at the expense of others. Real estate, construction deals, contracts that bypassed the usual channels. A lot of money changed hands."

A flicker of anger crossed Thorne's face, his eyes narrowing as he considered Haynes' words. "So Langston was pulling strings for people willing to pay?"

Haynes opened his mouth, then shut it, exhaling slowly. "It's not my place to speculate. All I know is that Langston operated on a different level. He liked being indispensable, and he wasn't shy about letting people know he held the cards."

His words painted a picture: Langston as the kingmaker, the man who dictated which projects would proceed, whose interests were worth protecting. People like him didn't just have rivals—they had enemies, people who resented the control he wielded. It made me wonder how many people were nursing grudges, watching from the sidelines as he flaunted his power.

Thorne took a step closer, his gaze unyielding. "Listen, Councilman, we're not here to drag you into this. But if you know something—if there's anything that can lead us to whoever did this—it's in your best interest to tell us now."

Haynes looked around, as if worried about hidden eyes or ears. "I heard rumors... of deals, contracts that vanished into thin air. If Langston was double-dealing, playing both sides... well, that makes him a target for more than just a few angry businessmen. But that's all they were. Rumors."

He didn't meet my gaze as he finished, his voice trailing off. There was a weight behind his words, something left unsaid. Thorne straightened, glancing at me, his expression hardening. We'd need more than whispers if we were going to crack this case open.

We left Haynes' office without another word, our footsteps echoing in the silence. Outside in the hallway, I glanced at Thorne. "It's all buried beneath layers of connections. The Spectator picked Langston for a reason. We need to find out why."

He nodded, his jaw set. "Then we start unraveling it, piece by piece."

Our next stop was with Patrick O'Connor, a journalist known for digging up dirt on the city's elite. I had reached out to him before, and he was reliable if slightly paranoid—a habit that came with the territory of exposing people with power.

We met him in a dingy bar on the outskirts of downtown, far from the gleaming towers that housed the people he regularly reported on. O'Connor was already nursing a drink when we arrived, his gaze darting around before he finally settled on us.

"Figured you'd come knocking sooner or later," he said, nodding for us to sit. "Langston's murder—it's got all the marks of something rotten under the surface."

"What do you know about him?" I asked, cutting straight to the point.

O'Connor chuckled, taking a long sip from his glass. "Langston was no choir boy, let's put it that way. He knew how to bend the rules, slip things under the radar. He's been at the center of a lot of dirty deals, but always had enough clout to stay clean. Or at least look that way."

Thorne's eyes sharpened. "And now he's dead. Think anyone in particular was unhappy with his deals?"

O'Connor shrugged, leaning back. "Hard to say. Could be anyone. Politicians, business execs, even a few big-money contractors who lost out on deals they thought were in the bag. Langston had this arrogance about him. Made enemies out of people who would've let things slide, if only he hadn't been so brazen."

I took in O'Connor's words, my mind racing through the list of possible suspects we were building. Each layer we uncovered revealed a darker, more tangled side of Langston's world. I felt a chill creep up my spine; if Langston was the Spectator's first target, there were likely more names on their list.

Thorne leaned forward, his voice low. "This Spectator, whoever they are, isn't just killing for personal vendettas. This feels... pointed. Political."

O'Connor's gaze flicked to the side, something shifting in his expression. "You're not wrong. The Spectator is making a statement, and it's got everyone who thinks they're untouchable looking over their shoulders."

He handed me a thin folder, his fingers tapping nervously on the table. "I've been keeping tabs on a few people Langston dealt with. Names, affiliations, deals they pushed through. Could be nothing. Could be something."

I flipped through the folder, scanning the names: developers, contractors, a few familiar faces from City Hall. Names that had come up before but never went anywhere. The pieces were all there, hidden in plain sight, waiting to be put together.

O'Connor finished his drink, setting his glass down with a hard clink. "This city has layers, Detective. The Spectator? They're pulling back the curtain, showing people what lies underneath. And if Langston's murder is just the start, then God help whoever's next."

We left the bar with O'Connor's folder in hand, our minds buzzing with the implications. Thorne looked over at me as we walked back to the precinct, his eyes steely.

"This isn't just murder, Emma. This is a reckoning," he said, voice grim. "And Langston was just the beginning."

Back at the precinct, I spread out the names and files from O'Connor's folder, each connection branching out like the twisted roots of a poisoned tree. Langston, Haynes, the developers, and several more names we hadn't even considered.

We had tapped into something deep and dangerous, a network of corruption that had festered beneath the city's polished surface for too long. Langston was merely a symptom of a larger disease, one that the Spectator seemed determined to expose, even if it meant leaving a trail of bodies in their wake.

As I stood back, surveying the tangled mess of names and motives, a cold realization settled in. The Spectator wasn't just killing—they were executing a plan, one that targeted the city's most powerful. And we were only beginning to scratch the surface.

I glanced at Thorne, who was staring at the wall of names with the same intensity. "The Spectator is sending a message," I said. "And they're making sure it's heard by everyone who matters."

He nodded, his gaze unwavering. "Then we'd better make sure we hear it first."

Chapter 4: A Cold Trail

The call came in just before dawn. The radio crackled with static, but the dispatcher's voice cut through loud and clear: another high-profile murder. I was in my car and halfway to the scene before the sun even touched the skyline. I could feel the adrenaline building, each heartbeat a reminder that the Spectator wasn't done yet.

Thorne joined me at the cordoned-off perimeter just as I arrived. His face was stone as he surveyed the scene, barely acknowledging the crowd of onlookers that had already gathered along the yellow tape. The victim's name was plastered across the news within minutes—Graham Keller, CEO of a multi-million-dollar contracting firm with deep ties to City Hall, and a man who held as much sway in the mayor's office as any elected official.

"What's the situation?" Thorne asked the officer on scene, his voice sharp.

The young officer shifted uncomfortably, nodding toward the high-rise building behind him. "Keller's penthouse. Building security says nobody came in or out all night, but somehow... well, he's dead. Same precision as Langston. Single gunshot wound to the head, close-range. But there's something else you should see."

We rode up the elevator to the top floor in silence, each floor ticked off by a mechanical beep that sounded almost like a countdown. Thorne and I had been here before, but this time, the sterile walls felt like a trap.

Inside, the penthouse was a study in excess: white leather couches, a floor-to-ceiling view of the skyline, polished surfaces reflecting every shard of the early morning light. But my eyes went immediately to the red smears near Keller's desk, where the forensic team had set up. The word "Spectator" was painted onto the glass wall in what looked like blood—a signature, just like at Langston's murder. A sickening calling card.

I moved closer, examining the scene. The message was clearer this time: *"Your time is up."* Three words, etched in a fluid line that seemed to taunt us. Keller had met his end with brutal efficiency, just like Langston. The Spectator's signature was unmistakable, a twisted blend of arrogance and calculation.

"What are we looking at here?" Thorne murmured, eyes flicking over the blood-spattered message.

"Not just another murder. This feels like... a warning," I said, my voice low. "Langston and now Keller. Two power players, both with connections that go deeper than we've seen on the surface. Whatever Keller was involved in, it's something worth killing for."

Thorne scanned the room, his gaze narrowing on the details: the expensive artwork, the untouched glass of scotch on the coffee table, Keller's open laptop, frozen on a spreadsheet full of figures and accounts. He crossed to the desk, tapping the keyboard, but the screen required a password.

"We'll need Sinclair to crack into his digital footprint," Thorne muttered. "Every little detail matters now."

Just then, Natalie Sinclair, our cyber-crime expert, strode in, a bag slung over her shoulder, her face set in determined focus. She'd been working on decrypting Langston's files, and the late hour hadn't deterred her.

"Looks like you've got another puzzle for me," she said, setting up her laptop on the desk beside Keller's. "I'll dig into his online transactions, his emails. If he was hiding anything, I'll find it."

"Anything specific we should be looking for?" I asked her, watching as her fingers flew across the keys.

"Patterns, links, strange bank transactions. Anything that looks like it's meant to stay buried," Sinclair replied. "Men like Keller don't keep secrets on paper. But even the smartest cover their tracks electronically."

As Sinclair worked, Thorne and I turned back to the crime scene. The Spectator had left little behind. No fingerprints, no hairs, no traceable residue—nothing that could give us a tangible lead. Just the chilling message and a perfect shot to the head, delivered with military precision.

While she worked, I scanned the surroundings, trying to reconstruct Keller's last moments. He'd likely been caught off guard, maybe even knew his killer. The penthouse door hadn't been forced, and the security system hadn't been tripped. It didn't fit. If this was politically motivated, as I suspected, the Spectator had inside knowledge, possibly someone with the kind of access that no one questions.

We found nothing of significance in the penthouse itself, and my frustration grew. Two murders, two elites. Different lives, but tied by a common thread of power. Keller's death didn't feel random, and the Spectator didn't seem like a simple vigilante. Each victim was chosen with intent, and I suspected the organization I'd only heard whispers of was the key to understanding it all.

Just then, Sinclair called us over. She'd managed to access Keller's financial records, and her face was pale as she studied the data. "There are some... peculiar transactions here. Large sums, sent through offshore accounts, all funneled back into a project listed under 'City Expansion'... except that project doesn't exist in any official files."

My stomach twisted. Keller and Langston weren't just corrupt—they were deeply embedded in something shadowy, something dangerous. "Could be hush money, or maybe a front for something larger," I suggested.

Thorne nodded grimly. "Black money. Whatever this is, it's big. And people are willing to kill to protect it."

I snapped on my gloves, returning to Keller's desk. Beneath a pile of receipts and invoices, I found a small key, hidden but not well enough for someone who knew what they were looking for. It was engraved with a serial number that didn't match any locks in his office. Something meant to be hidden away. I pocketed the key, noting to check for private storage facilities or off-site safes later. Keller's wealth and influence suggested he'd have places to stash things he didn't want anyone to find.

As I stood there, staring at the blood-red message on the glass, I couldn't shake the feeling that Keller and Langston were just the start. The Spectator's reach was growing, and we were chasing shadows down a dark corridor, each door leading to another question, another half-answer that dissolved as soon as it was within reach.

Sinclair looked up from her laptop, a frown creasing her forehead. "Detective, there's one more thing. A series of deleted emails... all to an encrypted account. The sender's ID is masked, but the domain's registered offshore. Whoever Keller was talking to didn't want anyone finding out."

Thorne and I exchanged a glance. A network of hidden communications, and now two high-profile deaths. The pieces were slowly slotting into place, revealing a conspiracy that spread far beyond simple political rivalries. And the Spectator? The Spectator was pulling the strings from behind a veil of secrecy, eliminating anyone who threatened their goals.

As we left the crime scene, I took a final look at the message on the glass. "Your time is up." It felt less like a warning and more like a sentence, spoken with the conviction of someone who believed themselves above the law. Whoever the Spectator was, they were only getting started, and unless we found a way to catch up, the city's elite would keep falling one by one.

Thorne's voice broke the silence as we headed back to the precinct. "Keller's murder proves that this isn't random. It's calculated, it's connected, and if we don't find a way in soon, there'll be another name on that list."

I clenched my fists, the weight of the case pressing down on me. The cold trail we were following wasn't just leading to the past—it was carving a path through the city's future, leaving destruction in its wake. And the only way to stop it was to get ahead of a ghost we could barely see.

Chapter 5: The Forensic Truth

The lab was quiet except for the faint hum of machines analyzing every detail of evidence Liam had collected from Keller's murder scene. A forensic sanctuary, it smelled of sterile air and lingering chemicals, a sharp contrast to the chaos of the crime itself. Dr. Liam Byrne, with his familiar focused expression, was hunched over his workstation, his dark eyes narrowed in concentration as he ran another set of tests.

He didn't look up as I entered, but he must have heard my footsteps. "Emma," he said, his tone grave. "You'll want to see this."

I approached, glancing at the data projected onto his screen—a detailed forensic breakdown of fibers, gunpowder traces, blood spatter angles. Liam pointed to a specific readout, his fingers hovering just above the screen. "The shot that killed Keller? Perfectly clean entry, minimal damage to surrounding tissue. The angle, the distance... this wasn't some hired thug's work. Whoever did this knew exactly what they were doing."

I studied the display, trying to absorb every detail. "Are we talking about someone with military experience?"

Liam tilted his head slightly. "Possible, but it's more specific than that. There's a precision here that goes beyond basic combat training. This is surgical. Almost clinical. It's like we're dealing with someone who's familiar with the inner workings of law enforcement, maybe even a seasoned professional."

I felt a chill crawl up my spine. The Spectator wasn't just a vigilante with a grudge against power; he—or she—had the kind of skill that suggested a background in law enforcement or intelligence. "Are there any traces? DNA? Hair? We need something that ties them to a physical identity."

Liam shook his head, lips pressed into a thin line. "Nothing that wasn't deliberately planted to throw us off. A stray hair here, partial fingerprints there—every piece of evidence left behind was a dead end. Almost as if they're taunting us. This person is meticulous. I've rarely seen anything like it."

My gaze shifted to the screens, where a digital image of Keller's blood-spattered desk remained frozen. Every splatter was preserved in high-definition, like an intricate, macabre map. Each stain told a story. I thought back to Langston's scene, to the blood-red message left scrawled on the glass. Both victims, both high-ranking and influential, taken down with a ruthlessness that bordered on surgical detachment.

"Anything in common between Langston's and Keller's deaths?" I asked, my voice low.

Liam tapped a few keys, pulling up Langston's autopsy results beside Keller's. "The method, the tools used, the way the crime scenes were left... this person knew we'd analyze every single detail. They left nothing to chance."

"So, we're looking for someone with training. Possibly someone with a law enforcement background. But why?" I frowned, a sense of unease settling over me. "What's the motive behind all this?"

Liam considered, his expression shadowed. "I don't think it's just power or revenge. This feels... personal, but not in the usual way. Whoever this is has a reason—a strong one—for what they're doing. And they're skilled enough to stay ahead of us every step of the way."

I took a deep breath, my mind running through every suspect we'd considered, every possible connection we'd examined. None of it fit. The Spectator was playing a game that was calculated down to the last move, and we were chasing shadows. The killer knew exactly how we'd react, how we'd try to decipher the clues left behind. It was a dance, and right now, they were leading.

Liam pulled up another screen, this time showing Keller's body. "Look at the wound here." He zoomed in on the single gunshot entry, clean and deliberate. "Most killers leave traces of hesitation, or there's a tell-tale difference in the way they handle the weapon. Not here. Whoever did this has the composure of a sniper, and the accuracy to match."

"That can't be just anyone," I muttered, my mind racing. "And it means they're prepared to go after anyone on their list, with little to no fear of being caught. They know we're chasing them, and they're watching us, playing us like pawns."

I could feel Liam's gaze as he studied my expression, searching for signs of doubt. "Emma, this isn't just a typical case. Whoever we're dealing with... they're not going to be easy to find."

"I know," I replied, gritting my teeth. "But that doesn't mean we're going to let them keep doing this."

Liam was quiet for a moment, the hum of machinery the only sound in the room. Finally, he pointed to the encrypted message found in Keller's emails—the one that Natalie Sinclair was working to decrypt. "If Sinclair can crack this, we might get a lead. It's the only thing we've got that could give us some insight into Keller's connections."

My phone buzzed, a notification from Sinclair herself. I read her message and felt a flicker of hope. She'd made progress on decoding Keller's communications, pulling out fragments of exchanges that hinted at a meeting in a location on the outskirts of the city, a remote warehouse often leased out by powerful businessmen looking for discretion.

I turned to Liam. "Sinclair found something. Keller was arranging meetings with someone—someone careful, who didn't want a digital trail. But they missed something, and we have a possible location to check out."

"Then we're getting closer," Liam said, his tone almost encouraging.

But as I stood there, a dark thought wormed its way into my mind. If the Spectator had this level of skill, this depth of knowledge about our own procedures, they'd have known we'd find Keller's emails. They might have planted this location as a trap, just like every other piece of evidence. Yet, what choice did we have? Every step brought us closer, even if we were stepping blindly into the unknown.

"I'll get Thorne," I said, heading toward the door. "We're checking out that warehouse. If there's anything there, we need to see it firsthand."

"Be careful," Liam said, his voice steady. "If this is a setup, you'll be walking straight into it."

I gave a curt nod. I knew the risks, but the need to find answers outweighed every warning. Each moment we spent hesitating was another moment the Spectator remained free to strike again, to pick another name off whatever list they were working through. The only thing left was to confront the shadows head-on, even if it meant walking through darkness.

Chapter 6: The Spectator's Message

The morning air felt thick, pressing down with an intensity that made each breath heavy. I'd barely had time to grab a coffee before my phone buzzed with an incoming message from Natalie Sinclair, our cyber-crime expert. Her tone, clipped and urgent, broke through my early morning haze.

"Emma," she said, "we have something new. You need to come down to tech, now."

Within minutes, I reached the sterile, blue-lit tech lab where Natalie was hunched over her computer, eyes trained on the screen as if the code itself might blink first. She glanced up as I approached, gesturing toward the screen. "The Spectator sent a message, direct to the precinct's secure line."

I raised an eyebrow, the weight of her words sinking in. "How secure are we talking?"

"Practically impenetrable," she replied. "Which means he's good. Very good."

On the screen, the email glowed against the dark background. The subject line read: *Message for the Observers.* A cryptic start, fittingly unnerving. Natalie clicked to open it, and I scanned the contents, my mind picking through every word as if it might hold the key to stopping whatever nightmare the Spectator had planned next.

The message read:

"To those who watch, remember that sight alone is never enough. The blind can often see more than those with open eyes. Soon, you'll understand. Soon, I'll make you see. For now, think of time as your enemy. When it runs out, the third falls."

The words were unsettlingly vague, every line crafted to taunt. It felt personal, a calculated jab that reminded us of just how powerless we were in this twisted game. The Spectator was playing on our turf now, crossing lines to prove a point—and somewhere, another target was likely being chosen.

"Did you trace it?" I asked, already half-knowing the answer.

Natalie shook her head, frustration evident in her clenched jaw. "The encryption is layered. Whoever this is, they know exactly how to cover their tracks. The email's been bounced across multiple servers, each route leading to dead ends. But..." She hesitated, then highlighted a string of numbers at the bottom of the message.

"This might mean something," she continued. "It's the only unique identifier left in the email, a deliberate signature. 9-6-3-4-8. Repeating twice."

I stared at the numbers, running them through my mind, searching for anything that clicked. "Is it a code? A sequence?"

"It's possible, or maybe a countdown," she replied, fingers tapping at her keyboard, calling up various databases to cross-reference the numbers. "But without context, it could be anything."

Inspector Jacob Thorne appeared in the doorway, his presence like a heavy weight added to the room. He scanned the message, his face darkening. "Another warning," he said. "And if this pattern holds, a third target's already lined up."

He turned to me, his gaze intent. "Emma, we need to break this before it escalates. Think. Could this be tied to any recent events?"

I ran through Keller and Langston's cases in my mind, every meeting, every suspicious contact. Each victim had their hands in city politics, deep enough to be entangled in the city's ugliest secrets. But that still didn't explain the numbers, or why the Spectator was taunting us with riddles instead of just striking again.

"Sinclair, try those numbers in every possible cross-reference," I said, my voice sharper than intended. The mounting tension seeped into my words. "Municipal records, personnel IDs, anything that connects them to City Hall or past events."

As she worked, I pulled Thorne aside. "There's more to this than simple revenge, Jacob. Every message, every strike—it's like the Spectator's trying to teach us something, forcing us to understand the why as much as the who."

Thorne's eyes hardened. "Then we have to be faster. If he's right, and time is our enemy, then every second wasted could cost another life."

Natalie suddenly straightened, her screen illuminating a possible connection. "Look at this," she called us over, displaying a list of events linked to the numbers. "City permits. They're coded with sequences that often include date markers."

"So these numbers might mark specific events?" I asked.

She nodded, scrolling through dates until she landed on one that made her freeze. "Nine-six. September sixth—two years ago. There was a city council hearing that day. Keller, Langston... they were both present. They were involved in a decision that transferred funding from a public housing initiative into private contracts."

Thorne let out a low whistle. "And that's a decision that would've made some powerful people very, very angry. It would explain the motive—if someone were deeply affected by that, financially or personally."

My mind raced, weaving possibilities. "The Spectator might be targeting people tied to that decision, making them pay for their part in it."

"But why now?" Thorne asked, his eyes narrowing. "What triggered this timing?"

Before I could respond, Natalie's computer pinged with a new notification—a second email. She opened it, and there, in the same taunting style, was another message:

"You're close, but sight is limited. Step beyond it, and perhaps you'll catch up. The third's fate lies in shadows cast by your own blindness. Look for what you've overlooked."

The message was signed with the same numerical code, 9-6-3-4-8, and below it, the words: *"The Spectator."*

An oppressive silence filled the room. I felt the gravity of his words pressing down, each phrase laced with both a threat and a challenge. We were close, but not close enough. And the Spectator knew that, playing off our limitations with infuriating precision.

"I'll be damned," Thorne muttered. "He's practically giving us the tools, but every hint sends us back into a maze."

I looked over at Natalie, who seemed as tense as I felt. "Have there been any recent city permits issued with this same numerical structure?"

She typed furiously, scanning the most recent records. After a few seconds, she turned the screen toward us, her face pale. "There's a meeting scheduled for tonight—another council gathering with Keller and Langston's associates. Every name here is linked to that original transfer decision."

My heart pounded. The Spectator wasn't just hinting at a third target—he was orchestrating another strike in plain sight. Tonight's gathering was his stage, and every person attending was a potential victim.

"Emma, if we don't move now," Thorne's voice was sharp, slicing through my thoughts. "He'll strike again before we even get close."

I nodded, already heading toward the door. "Then let's make sure we're there before he gets the chance."

I pulled out my phone, calling for every available officer to head toward City Hall. Time had always been our enemy, but now it was a tangible countdown ticking toward a third murder. Every step toward the precinct door felt heavy with urgency.

And yet, in the back of my mind, I couldn't shake the feeling that the Spectator was leading us exactly where he wanted.

Chapter 7: Tangled Webs

The office felt oppressively quiet as the evidence board in front of me filled with familiar faces, names, red strings connecting them like the veins of a malignant beast. The more we unraveled, the more I could feel something lurking behind it all—a dark pulse threading through the city's halls of power. The faces of Keller and Langston were side by side, staring back at me from their police profile photos, reminders of a chain we hadn't yet broken. Each of them had held influence—Keller in finance, Langston in policy reform—but those were just the surface titles.

Thorne entered, balancing two mugs of coffee, his gaze following mine toward the board. He held out a mug, his usual offering when he could sense I was drowning in my thoughts. "Late-night epiphany, or just insomnia?"

I took the mug, barely feeling the warmth, as my eyes stayed glued to the board. "It's not adding up, Jacob. The more we dig, the more it feels like a setup. Every trail feels planted, almost too easy—like we're following breadcrumbs."

He nodded, stepping closer to inspect the tangled mess of connections we'd laid out. "Every victim wielded influence, that's for sure. But it's too spread out. Politicians, businesspeople... if there's a reason they're being taken down, it's hidden deeper than we've looked so far."

I exhaled, nodding. "It's not just who they were, but what they represented. These are people who shifted policy, swayed public funds, backed profitable ventures. And there are ties..." I pointed to a new addition to the board, the string connecting Langston to a high-ranking city official in the mayor's office, a link we'd uncovered just that morning. "Langston had connections that went deeper than we knew—contracts funneled through silent partners, public projects that turned private under his watch. If he was involved in any illegal dealings, he would've been valuable."

"Valuable enough to silence?" Thorne's question hung in the air, heavy and pointed.

Before I could respond, Natalie walked in, a laptop under her arm. She placed it on the table, her face tense with the energy of someone who'd just unlocked something important. "I traced more than the usual in Langston's financials, and the deeper I went, the more it felt like I was peeling back layers of a rotten onion. Accounts linked to offshore holdings, transactions with unlisted corporations, a maze of shell companies. It's bigger than just a few bribes."

She opened the laptop, the screen filling with financial data, each entry dripping with dark implications. "The Spectator's targets weren't just influencers; they were players in a game the rest of us barely glimpse. The question is... who's holding the rulebook?"

Thorne ran a hand over his face, frustration evident. "If the Spectator is targeting people with a certain level of corruption, this won't be a short list. This city's power players cover every facet of influence, every corner of the elite."

I studied the board, trying to connect one more elusive dot that danced just out of reach. "What if," I started slowly, "the Spectator's targets aren't random, but meticulously planned—each victim a stepping stone, leading us toward someone or something bigger? What if they're not the top of the chain but just the beginning?"

Natalie tapped her finger on the screen. "That makes sense. Think about it. The killings are public, high-profile enough to grab the media's attention, which means it's likely a setup for something larger. The Spectator isn't looking to be a serial killer; he's looking to prove a point, expose someone—or something."

A strange chill crept through me. "Then he's taunting us because he knows we're close. Or maybe... maybe we're not even looking at the right suspects."

My phone buzzed on the desk, jolting me from my train of thought. A text from Ryan Fitzgerald, a streetwise informant I'd leaned on for the grittier parts of this city's network. His message was brief but potent: *"Meet me in person. There's talk you need to hear."*

I met Thorne's gaze, showing him the message. "Fitzgerald wants to meet. If he's reaching out like this, it's something major."

Fifteen minutes later, I was standing in a dingy alleyway, the city's hum muffling the sounds of our conversation. Fitzgerald's eyes darted around before he spoke, his voice low and cautious.

"Word is, your case isn't just ruffling feathers—it's tearing down nests," he said, his gaze shifting toward the shadows as if expecting them to whisper secrets back. "The people you're looking into... they're deep in this city's veins, right up to the mayor's office."

I leaned in, my voice steady. "Tell me something I don't know, Fitzgerald. If I wanted vague warnings, I could've stayed in my office."

He clenched his jaw, frustration flickering in his eyes. "Alright, then. How about this? There's talk that Keller and Langston were covering for someone high up, running deals that weren't just for their own pockets. They were messengers, conduits, doing the dirty work for bigger players. And if the Spectator's hitting people with those ties, there's a list longer than you'd like to think."

His words hit like a sledgehammer. This wasn't just about power or money. We were in the middle of something woven through the city's core, a network as tangled and rotted as the secrets it held. "Who are the bigger players? Names, Ryan. I need names."

He hesitated, looking down, his voice barely above a whisper. "Jessica Walker. She's the gatekeeper, the prosecutor who plays both sides. She's one of the few who's walked that line without getting caught. But she's more involved than anyone wants to believe."

Jessica Walker. The prosecutor we'd relied on for so many cases, a name I'd thought I could trust. If she was involved in this network, the case was darker than I'd dared to imagine.

Ryan's eyes flashed with urgency. "You didn't hear that from me. The people I just mentioned? They're dangerous. They'll tear you apart if they catch even a whisper of your digging."

I nodded, the weight of his words pressing down like a storm cloud. As he disappeared into the shadows, his warning echoed in my mind. Trust was becoming a scarce commodity, each ally a potential enemy in a game with no clear end.

When I returned to the precinct, Thorne's gaze followed me as I entered the room, a question in his eyes. "What did Fitzgerald say?"

I hesitated, my pulse pounding with the implications. "He gave us a name," I said slowly. "Jessica Walker."

Thorne's face twisted, disbelief flickering over his features. "Walker? She's one of us."

I felt the same disbelief clawing at me, a betrayal inching closer with every word. "I know. But according to Fitzgerald, she's been playing a double game, handling cases that allow certain... influences to stay untouched."

We shared a look, both recognizing the depth of the betrayal if this lead turned out to be true. Jessica Walker had held our trust, defended our cases, seen the ugly underbelly of every investigation we brought her way. And now, it seemed, she might be part of that same underbelly.

Natalie was still at her laptop, sifting through records, oblivious to the storm that was gathering between Thorne and me. I took a deep breath, setting my focus back on the case. "Let's double-check everything she's touched. If Walker's involved, there's got to be a trail she didn't cover."

Thorne nodded, a grim resolve settling over him. "And if we find something?"

"We confront her. If she's hiding anything, I want to see it in her eyes."

I turned back to the evidence board, each name and connection now carrying the weight of potential betrayal. The deeper we went, the less clear the lines between friend and foe became. But one thing was certain: the Spectator had torn open the city's secrets, forcing us to face the tangled web beneath.

And as I stared at Jessica Walker's photo on the board, I knew we were just beginning to understand the scale of the darkness surrounding us.

Chapter 8: The Journalist's Perspective

I stood by the window, the weight of the case pressing down like a fog, thick and suffocating. The city was beginning to wake up, its streets alive with the usual rush, but inside this room, it felt like the world had slowed to a crawl. The names on the board blurred together, each piece of evidence leading nowhere clear, each step forward dragging us deeper into a murky abyss.

The door to the office swung open, breaking my concentration. I turned, my hand instinctively resting on the sidearm holstered at my hip. Patrick O'Connor stepped in, his presence as abrupt as his arrival. His trench coat was still damp from the rain outside, his eyes sharp and determined, a glint of ambition in the way he moved. O'Connor wasn't one to wait for an invitation. He never had been.

"Detective Woodward," he said, his voice smooth but edged with impatience. "I hope I'm not interrupting anything too important."

I kept my distance, watching him carefully. O'Connor wasn't the type to walk into a room without purpose. The investigative journalist had his own methods, methods that often skirted the law in favor of getting a story—getting the truth out, no matter the cost. I hadn't decided yet if I liked him or if I was just wary of him.

"You're not interrupting," I said, my tone neutral. "What's on your mind, O'Connor?"

He flashed a quick smile, though I didn't return it. The man was too used to getting what he wanted. "I've been following the Spectator case," he began, setting a folder down on the table between us. "I think I might have some information that could help you." He tapped the folder, leaning in slightly as though the contents were a secret only for me.

I eyed him. "I didn't ask for your help, O'Connor."

He didn't flinch. "You're not exactly getting anywhere without it. I've got sources—people on the inside. People who know things you might not. If we put our heads together, maybe we can start connecting the dots."

I didn't say anything right away. The idea of working with him made my skin crawl. I had seen enough of his articles—his willingness to cross lines to get the story, to make alliances with people whose motives were less than pure. He wasn't a traditional journalist, by any means. He was an opportunist, willing to bend the rules as long as the story served his own interests.

I could feel his gaze on me, waiting for an answer. I crossed my arms over my chest, leaning back in my chair, keeping my expression as unreadable as possible.

"What do you think the Spectator is after?" I asked, trying to steer the conversation, to get a sense of whether his angle was anything close to relevant.

He didn't hesitate. "The killings? They're part of something much bigger. You're looking at them as isolated incidents—just a few high-profile murders, and that's it. But I think they're connected to the city's corruption. The Spectator, he's not just cleaning house. He's sending a message. A warning."

I scoffed, half amused. "A warning to who? The mayor? The council? This city's full of dirty hands, O'Connor. A hundred different people could fit the profile of the Spectator's next target."

"Exactly." He tapped his fingers on the table, leaning in closer. "Which is why you need to see the bigger picture. These murders aren't random. The people he's choosing have power—power that controls the very systems this city runs on. There's a pattern to the chaos, and the more you ignore it, the more you risk missing the point."

I felt my pulse quicken, despite myself. "And what's the point?" I asked, my voice sharper now.

"The point," O'Connor said, his eyes gleaming, "is that these murders are the beginning of something much more than just a rogue killer taking out corrupt politicians and businessmen. These murders are a direct challenge to the entire system. And I think you're missing the most important part—who's actually pulling the strings."

I narrowed my eyes. "What are you implying?"

He leaned back, folding his arms as though the weight of his information was a burden. "You're too close to it, Woodward. You've been investigating from the inside, trusting the law and the people within it. But that's the problem. The system itself is rotten. People are watching you. Your every move. You're just one piece of the puzzle, one part of the story. But you're not seeing the whole picture."

His words hung heavy in the room. The sense of unease crawled through my veins again. Was he onto something, or was this just another attempt to get ahead of a story? He didn't have any real proof, just insinuation and thin threads of suspicion. But I couldn't ignore the way he made me feel—like I was missing something, something crucial.

"I don't work with people who think they can solve a case just by guessing the right narrative," I said, pushing the folder back toward him. "If you have real evidence, O'Connor, then present it. Otherwise, we're done here."

His smile faltered, but only for a second. He didn't take the bait. Instead, he slid the folder back across the table, stopping it just short of my hand. "Fine. You want evidence? I've got sources who've been feeding me information. I've been digging into political connections, digging into the mayor's office. There's more going on here than you think. But you're going to need my help if you want to connect the dots."

I hesitated. I didn't want to admit it, but the weight of the case was beginning to feel unbearable. It was starting to feel like I wasn't just chasing a killer anymore. I was chasing a ghost, and every step forward only led to deeper shadows. The connections were becoming harder to untangle, the names and faces on the board blurring together like a twisted game I couldn't understand.

I took a slow breath, my fingers brushing the folder before I picked it up. "You have one chance, O'Connor. One. If you cross the line, if I find out you're playing me, you're out. And I won't hesitate to make sure you never work in this city again."

His eyes never wavered, and for the first time, I saw something like respect in his gaze. "I don't need to play you, Woodward. I just need you to see the truth."

I flipped open the folder, the papers inside filled with information I'd seen before but through a different lens. Patterns, names, connections—everything O'Connor had uncovered and was now offering to me.

As I scanned the details, my mind worked furiously to connect the dots. This wasn't a coincidence. The deeper I looked, the more I saw the fractures in the system—fractures that led straight back to the people in power. O'Connor's theory was flawed, but there was a kernel of truth buried beneath his words.

For now, I had no choice but to trust him. But I'd be watching closely. In this game, trust was a currency I couldn't afford to spend too easily.

"Alright," I said, my voice steady. "Let's see what you've got."

O'Connor's smile returned, but it didn't reach his eyes. He knew as well as I did that this was just the beginning.

Chapter 9: A Target in Plain Sight

The phone rang, slicing through the silence of my office. I didn't need to look at the caller ID. It was Lieutenant Ramirez again. I picked it up, already knowing what she was going to say.

"It's a judge, Emma. A third murder."

I felt my pulse quicken as I stood, pushing my chair back with a creak. "Who?"

"Judge Harold Winters. The one who's been making waves with his anti-corruption rulings. He's dead."

I dropped my hand to the desk, trying to steady myself. Winters was a significant figure, known for his no-nonsense stance against corruption. His rulings had rocked the political foundations of this city. If the Spectator had him in his sights, we were dealing with something much bigger than I had originally thought.

"I'm on my way," I said, disconnecting the call.

I grabbed my coat, my mind racing. Three murders, three prominent figures, each tied to corruption in some way. This wasn't a random spree. It was calculated, methodical. The Spectator wasn't just picking targets; he was playing a game. And we were always a step behind.

By the time I arrived at the scene, the area was already swarming with officers and forensic teams. The bright flashing lights of the squad cars cast an eerie glow against the darkened street, but the crowd of onlookers had already begun to dissipate, their curiosity already sated by the grisly scene. I felt the weight of the city's eyes on me. They expected answers. They wanted justice. But we were nowhere near that.

"Over here, Detective."

I turned toward Ramirez, who was standing near the entrance of Winters' penthouse. She was visibly tense, her expression hard as stone. She didn't need to say anything more; her face told me everything.

I followed her inside.

The apartment was lavish, reflecting the wealth Winters had accumulated during his years on the bench. Expensive artwork lined the walls, and a grand piano sat in the corner, untouched, its keys silent. But none of that mattered now. What mattered was the body lying on the floor, surrounded by a pool of blood that had long since dried.

Winters' face was frozen in a grimace, his eyes wide open in shock, but it wasn't the expression that caught my attention. It was the method of the murder. His hands were bound behind his back, his legs splayed apart. The body was posed deliberately, just like the others.

I stepped closer, scanning the room. There was no sign of forced entry. The killer had come and gone without leaving a trace. The only thing that stood out was a single item on the coffee table in front of the judge: a black envelope. My stomach dropped.

I reached for it, my gloved hand trembling slightly as I turned it over. The seal was unbroken. I knew exactly what it was before I even opened it.

Inside was a single sheet of paper, the text typed in clean, precise letters. It read:

"The judge may have ruled against the system, but he forgot the most important rule: nothing escapes the eye of the Spectator."

I felt a chill race up my spine. The message was direct. And chilling. The Spectator had just taken down someone who had publicly opposed corruption, someone who had been working to expose the very system we were all tangled in.

"What does this mean, Emma?" Ramirez asked, her voice tight with frustration.

I didn't answer right away. My mind was racing. The judge's murder wasn't random. It had been planned. The Spectator knew exactly what he was doing. The message, the precision of the kill—it all pointed to someone with a deep understanding of how power worked in this city.

"The method," I said, finally finding my voice. "It's almost like... the killer is teaching us something. Each one of these victims represents a piece of the system, and the Spectator is systematically dismantling it."

"You think this is personal?"

"I don't know yet. But it feels like we're being played," I replied. "Like it's a game, and the killer's always two moves ahead of us."

I turned to Ramirez, my eyes scanning the room. The more I thought about it, the more I realized how little we actually knew. There were too many questions and not enough answers. We had no idea where the killer would strike next. And worse, we were running out of time.

"We need to find out who is connected to Winters. Who might have wanted him dead," I said, already walking toward the door. "We can't afford to wait. The Spectator isn't just targeting random people. He's targeting those who have the power to change things."

We left the apartment, and as I stepped out into the cold air, a sense of urgency washed over me. We were too far behind, and the killer was getting closer to whatever endgame he had in mind. I couldn't shake the feeling that we were being watched. The pressure was building, and each day that passed without a breakthrough only made it worse.

Back at the precinct, I met with Thorne and the rest of the team to go over Winters' background. His anti-corruption efforts had made him a number of enemies, both in the business world and in politics. The list of suspects was long, but that was no longer the issue. The issue was finding the connection between them all.

The killer was methodical. He didn't leave loose ends. And right now, we were the loose end. I could feel it in the pit of my stomach: we were the target now, whether we realized it or not.

Thorne glanced at me as I flipped through Winters' case files, his voice steady but filled with concern. "What are we missing, Emma?"

I didn't have an answer for him. I wanted to believe we could catch the Spectator before he killed again. But the truth was, every step we took, we only found more questions, and fewer answers.

"This isn't just a murder case anymore," I said quietly, my fingers tightening around the file. "This is a war. And we're playing catch-up."

I closed the file, the frustration eating at me. The pieces of the puzzle were there, but the picture was still out of focus. It wasn't enough to just follow the killer's trail. We needed to think like him, anticipate his moves. But for now, it felt like we were the ones running scared.

The Spectator was winning. And I didn't know how much longer we had before he made his next move.

Chapter 10: The Digital Footprint

I wasn't ready for Natalie Sinclair. I had heard about her before—rumors, mostly—but seeing her in action was something else entirely. She was calm, precise, and moved with an air of confidence that made her seem like she was always ten steps ahead of everyone else. She was the kind of person who could pull secrets from the digital ether like they were nothing, and we needed that. Fast.

"Emma, Thorne," she greeted us with a tight smile as we entered the room. Her eyes were already scanning the array of monitors in front of her. "I've gone through the encrypted emails and messages. Someone's been busy."

I took a seat next to her, and Thorne stood a bit farther away, arms crossed, watching the screen as she typed furiously. She didn't look up, her fingers dancing over the keyboard as if she knew exactly what she was doing.

"What have you found?" I asked, trying to sound casual, though my voice betrayed my impatience.

"Several things," she said, finally pulling up a list of files. "First, there's the message we found at the scene of the judge's murder. That wasn't the first one. This killer has been sending out encrypted messages to specific people in the city for months."

"Months?" Thorne raised an eyebrow, stepping closer.

"Yes," Natalie replied. "They go back as far as the first victim, the politician. What we've got here is a pattern, but it's layered, and unless you have a background in cryptography, it's nearly impossible to understand on your own."

She brought up a series of email headers and message fragments, most of them looking like gibberish. Strings of numbers and letters that appeared completely random.

"The Spectator's been laying the groundwork for a while," she continued. "These messages have been carefully hidden in public forums, dark web sites, and even social media channels that most people don't think to look at. The killer's creating a digital trail, but it's like a spider web—small, fragile, but if you look long enough, you can see how everything connects."

"How are we supposed to connect the dots if it's all encrypted?" I asked, trying to make sense of the screen in front of me. The letters danced around like they were mocking me.

"That's where I come in," Natalie said, a small, self-assured smile curling at her lips. She opened another program, a decryption tool, and in seconds, the cryptic messages began to appear in clear text.

"I found a few basic patterns in the encoding. The Spectator's been using a variety of methods to hide messages, including base64 encoding, simple ciphers, and even steganography. Some of these messages are embedded in images. It's like playing a game, but every piece of the puzzle is hidden in plain sight."

I leaned forward, focusing on the screen. Words began to form from the chaotic jumble of letters. They weren't just random messages—they were instructions. There was a distinct sense of purpose in the way the killer communicated. Each message felt like a challenge, like a game of cat and mouse.

"The Spectator isn't just communicating with us. He's taunting us. It's almost like a scavenger hunt," Natalie explained, zooming in on one particular message.

The text on the screen read:

"One step closer, but you're still looking in the wrong places. A false trail leads to a darker truth."

I felt a knot form in my stomach. The message was clear. We were being led somewhere, but not to the right place. Someone was controlling the narrative, and it wasn't us.

"That's not all," Natalie said, opening a new file. "There's more. Look here."

She pulled up a map of the city, a grid-like structure with several marked locations. Some were familiar to me—places I had been to, spots that were close to the heart of the city's political power. But some of them were obscure, tucked away in neighborhoods I wouldn't normally think to look.

"There's a pattern to these locations," she said, zooming in on one that caught my attention. "This one is at the edge of the city. And this one... it's in an abandoned building, close to the river."

Thorne stepped forward, his brow furrowing. "What does this mean?"

"It means the Spectator is laying out the next phase of his plan. He's marking the spots where he's going to strike next," Natalie said, her voice even but tense. "We just don't know what exactly he's going to do."

I was silent for a moment, staring at the locations. The messages, the digital footprint—it was all coming together, but the pieces were fragmented. Something wasn't right, and I couldn't quite put my finger on it.

Natalie kept scrolling, revealing more encrypted files, but I felt the weight of the situation settling on me. Every second we wasted was another second the Spectator was out there, watching, planning. We had to move fast, but I also knew that we were already in his game. He had the upper hand.

"This killer is smart," I said, more to myself than to anyone else. "He's not just some random murderer. He knows how to cover his tracks. And he knows how to play with us."

Thorne leaned against the table, running his hands through his hair. "We've been chasing shadows for too long. It feels like we're not getting closer to the truth, just further from it."

"We are," I replied. "But we're also closer than we think. If we can break these codes, if we can follow the digital trail, maybe we can get to the Spectator before he makes his next move."

Natalie tapped a few more keys, and a new screen popped up. A file was open, one that hadn't been decrypted yet. It was a long string of numbers, almost like coordinates. My pulse quickened as I stared at the screen, and I could feel the tension in the room rise. This wasn't just a message. It was something more. A clue, hidden deep within the killer's encrypted world.

"We need to check this out," I said, standing up abruptly. "Now."

Thorne was already grabbing his coat. Natalie nodded, her expression unreadable but focused. We weren't just dealing with a killer anymore; we were dealing with someone who was using the digital world as a weapon. And right now, it felt like the weapon was pointed directly at us.

As we headed for the door, I couldn't shake the feeling that someone was watching us. The Spectator was out there, somewhere, lurking in the shadows of the digital world, waiting for his next move.

Chapter 11: Uncovering the Past

I've spent my entire life trying to outrun my past. That's the thing about secrets—they always find their way back. They have a way of slinking into the corners of your mind, and just when you think they're buried, they rise again.

The case had already taken everything I had. The pressure, the long nights, the fear gnawing at the edges of my thoughts. I had buried so much of myself under the weight of my badge, but the deeper I went into the Spectator's world, the more I realized that it was impossible to keep my past and present separated. The lines blurred. My past was coming back to haunt me in ways I couldn't ignore.

It started with the phone call. It was an unfamiliar number, one I didn't recognize, but when I saw the name on the screen, my heart sank.

"Emma, it's your father. We need to talk."

I didn't answer right away. I hadn't heard from him in over a year. Maybe longer. There was always something about that man—something cold that made it impossible for me to hold onto any sense of warmth. He was a man who lived in the shadows, and I had always been his biggest disappointment.

I let the phone ring out. He wasn't calling to apologize. Not for anything.

Thorne noticed my distraction as I stared at the phone in my hand. I could tell he saw the tension in my face, the way I clenched my fist around the device. He didn't ask questions—he didn't need to. He already knew there were things I hadn't shared, things I was running from.

"Everything okay?" he asked, though his voice lacked the warmth of concern. It was more like a statement than a question.

"Yeah," I said quickly, hitting the end call button and sliding the phone back into my pocket. "Just... family stuff."

Thorne didn't press further, and I was grateful for it. He knew when not to ask.

We'd been going through the evidence all morning—Natasha had dug deeper into the encrypted messages from the Spectator, and Thorne had started to make calls. But there was something gnawing at me, something about the case that felt too familiar.

When I stepped outside for a break, the city felt suffocating. The air was thick, and the cold pressed against my skin. It was like walking through a fog.

I was walking in circles, trying to clear my head, but no matter how fast my feet moved, the past kept catching up with me. I hadn't thought about my father in months—years, even. But now, with every step I took toward solving the case, the memory of him loomed larger. I knew I couldn't ignore it. I had to face it, if only to move forward.

My father was a businessman, but that wasn't all he was. He had ties to the city's political world—deep ties. Ties I never asked about because, growing up, I was always told to stay away. Never ask questions. Never look too deep.

But now, I couldn't shake the feeling that the Spectator's killings were more than just a random act of revenge or corruption. There was a method to it, a pattern that, somehow, connected to my father. Or, more likely, to the things I had never allowed myself to dig into—the things I had spent my whole life ignoring.

I went home that night, feeling the weight of it all. The case. My father. The endless parade of unanswered questions. The sound of the door clicking behind me felt like the final barrier between myself and the rest of the world. But there was no escape, not tonight.

The phone rang again, and this time, I answered.

"Emma, I don't have much time," my father's voice said, gravelly and urgent. "We need to talk. You're in danger. They're looking for you."

My stomach dropped. I didn't ask who 'they' were. I didn't need to.

I could feel the heat rising in my chest, the anger bubbling beneath the surface. "What do you mean, 'danger'? What's going on?"

"Listen to me, Emma," he continued, his voice lowering to a near whisper. "The Spectator... it's all tied to me. To us. You've been chasing ghosts. And now you've become one of them."

I felt the words hit like a punch to the gut. The Spectator? Tied to my family? It didn't make sense. But the more I listened, the more I realized how little I actually knew about my father's past.

He didn't give me answers, only cryptic warnings and half-truths. But I knew, deep down, that there was more to this than he was willing to admit.

The call ended abruptly, leaving me standing in the middle of the room, phone still pressed to my ear. My thoughts were racing. I had to keep my head in the game. The Spectator was out there, and I couldn't afford distractions. But how could I ignore the fact that everything—the victims, the clues, the murders—seemed to be drawing a direct line back to my family?

The next morning, I made a decision. I couldn't let this case consume me and cloud my judgment any longer. I would dig into my past. I would uncover the truth, no matter how ugly it was. Because only then could I stop the Spectator from continuing his reign of terror.

Thorne and I met early, going over the latest developments in the case. But even as we discussed leads, my mind was elsewhere. I couldn't focus on the Spectator alone anymore. My past had become too big to ignore.

Thorne noticed my distraction. He didn't push me this time. He knew something was wrong. Something deeper than just a case.

"You don't have to do this alone, Emma," he said quietly, leaning over the table, his gaze softening just slightly. "Whatever's going on, we'll handle it. Together."

I nodded, feeling a lump form in my throat. But there was no time for emotion, not now. There were people to catch, and time was running out.

As we moved forward, the line between my past and the investigation became more tangled, like a rope pulling tighter, choking the air from my lungs. My history, my family's secrets, and the Spectator—they were all pieces of the same puzzle. I just had to figure out how they all fit together before it was too late.

Chapter 12: The Informant's Call

The phone rang, breaking the silence of my office, and my instincts told me that this wasn't just another update on the case. The tone was different, urgent—almost too urgent. I hesitated for a second, fingers hovering over the receiver, before picking up.

"Detective Woodward?" A gravelly voice crackled through the line.

"Yes?" I tried to place the voice but couldn't.

"You don't know me, but I know you. I've got information on the Spectator."

The words hit like a slap to the face. No one had come forward like this before. It felt like something was shifting, but I couldn't tell if it was an opportunity or a trap.

"Who is this?" I asked, my voice steady, though my gut churned.

"Ryan Fitzgerald," the man said. "I used to be an informant for the department. You can check me out if you want, but I'm guessing you're already doing that. I know who the Spectator is. I've been following him for months."

I stood, walking over to the window. The city below me looked still, like a machine stuck in place. But the noise in my head? It was anything but still. Every word Ryan said made my pulse race faster.

"You have my attention," I said carefully, keeping my voice neutral. "Why now? Why come forward?"

"Because it's getting dangerous. I'm not the only one he's after, Woodward. And I've seen the signs. It's only a matter of time before he comes for me, too."

"Why should I believe you?" I couldn't help but ask. This could be a game. A lie to get my attention. To get something out of me. I'd learned the hard way not to trust anyone who showed up out of nowhere, especially someone like Ryan Fitzgerald, a former criminal informant with a long history of bending the truth to his advantage.

"I'm not asking you to believe me," Ryan's voice was calm, too calm. "I'm asking for protection. You want the Spectator? You protect me. That's the deal."

My mind raced. The idea of working with someone like Ryan felt wrong. He had his own agenda, his own reasons for being involved in this mess. But the Spectator? The more I thought about it, the more his name came back to me, echoing in my mind. This could be the break we needed, or it could be the bait for a trap.

"What do you know?" I asked, keeping my tone firm.

"I know who he is. I've seen the pattern. He's been leaving clues, taunting you. The cryptic emails, the timing of the murders. I know what it means. But if you want this to go anywhere, I need you to give me some protection. I can't go to the cops, not after what happened last time. You're my only shot."

I rubbed my temples, the tension in my body growing. This wasn't simple. Nothing about this case had been simple. And now, this informant, this man with ties to the criminal world, was asking me to trust him? My instincts were screaming at me to back off, to shut him down before this spiraled out of control.

"Why should I protect you?" I asked, every word measured. "You're not exactly in the department's good graces, Fitzgerald. You've burned your bridges."

"That's why I'm asking for protection," Ryan shot back quickly. "The people I used to work with are out for blood. I've been hiding for months. I'm not in a good place, Woodward, but I can help you stop this."

There was a pause, a silence so thick it almost suffocated the words that hung between us. I wanted to end the call. I wanted to dismiss him as another liar, but something in his tone made me hesitate.

"I need to know who the Spectator is," I said, after a beat. "I need proof that you're not playing me."

"Come meet me. I'll give you the proof. But I'm not doing it over the phone, and I'm not doing it anywhere near the department. You get me protection, you get the information. Otherwise, I'm out. Simple as that."

I exhaled slowly, frustration building in my chest. There were too many unknowns here. Too many risks. But I didn't have a choice. The Spectator was out there, and if there was even a chance that Ryan had information that could help, I had to follow through.

"Where?" I asked, trying to push down the unease.

"St. Mark's Park. Midnight. Don't be late, Woodward."

The line went dead before I could respond.

I stared at the phone for a long moment, the words echoing in my mind. St. Mark's Park. Midnight. Why did that sound like a trap?

"Thorne," I muttered to myself. I needed backup. But this wasn't something I could tell him over the phone. If Ryan had information, I couldn't risk scaring him off. And I couldn't afford to go in unprepared.

I turned toward my desk, gathering my notes on the case. The pattern was starting to take shape, but it was still too fragmented. And now, this. Another piece of the puzzle—or another twisted game in the making?

I had to find out. For better or for worse, I was going to meet Ryan Fitzgerald at St. Mark's Park. And I had to be ready for whatever he was about to reveal—or whatever trap he was about to set.

Later that night, I stood at the edge of St. Mark's Park, the city lights barely reaching into the darkness. The air was cold, sharp enough to cut through the layers of my jacket. The park felt abandoned, every rustle of leaves amplified in the silence. I couldn't shake the feeling that I was being watched.

I glanced at my watch—11:58. Two minutes.

And then, I heard the footsteps.

Footsteps that didn't belong to me.

Ryan Fitzgerald stepped into view, his face hidden under the hood of his jacket, his movements quick, deliberate. But something about him—something about the way he held himself—told me he wasn't alone.

"I'm here," he said, his voice low, as he stopped a few feet away from me.

I didn't move.

"Where's the information?" I asked, keeping my voice steady, despite the growing tension in the pit of my stomach.

"You'll get it," Ryan said, but there was something in his eyes—something off. "But not here."

Before I could respond, a figure stepped out of the shadows, and everything inside me screamed to move. But it was too late.

Chapter 13: The Hunter Becomes the Hunted

The night air was thick with the weight of everything I had just seen. Ryan Fitzgerald had been nothing more than a decoy. The figure that stepped from the shadows was no ordinary thug—it was the Spectator, and he had been watching us the whole time. I could feel the chill in the air, as if every breath I took was an accusation. My instincts screamed at me to run, but I was frozen, locked in place by the realization that everything had changed.

Ryan made a sudden move, as if to step forward, but the figure with him raised a gloved hand, signaling him to stop. A sharp laugh echoed in the night. It was low, chilling, and undeniably confident. The Spectator knew what was happening. He knew where we were. And I realized then that I wasn't the one hunting anymore. The hunter had become the hunted.

"Emma Woodward," the figure spoke, his voice smooth but laced with an undertone of mockery. "You've been busy, haven't you?"

My mind raced as I struggled to process what was unfolding in front of me. How had he known? How could he be here, right now, right where I had planned to meet Ryan? My gut twisted with fear, but I didn't show it. Not yet.

"Don't play games," I said, my voice cutting through the stillness of the night. "What do you want?"

The Spectator stepped closer, the shadows almost swallowing him whole as he emerged from the darkness. His face was hidden under a black mask, but his presence was overwhelming. He was confident—too confident.

"You've been searching for me for so long," he said. "But you've missed every step along the way. The game is not yours to win, Detective. It never was."

I took a step back, my hand instinctively brushing the gun at my hip. A flicker of movement caught my eye—Ryan was backing away, his expression filled with regret. He was a rat, a man who had led me into this mess.

"What do you want?" I asked again, my voice stronger this time, though I could feel the pulse of fear rising in my chest.

The Spectator tilted his head as if considering the question. "I've already told you. I want you to see the truth. I want you to understand that all of this—this city, these people, your precious little system—is a lie. They've been lying to you all along, Detective. I'm just the one who's brave enough to show you."

My grip on the gun tightened, but I kept my hands steady. He was playing mind games, trying to rattle me. He wanted a reaction.

"I'm not afraid of you," I said, my voice steady, though I could feel the cold sweat starting to form on the back of my neck. I didn't believe my own words, but I needed him to hear them. "And I will stop you."

A laugh bubbled from beneath the mask. "You think you're the one in control here? You think you're the one who can stop me? You're already too late."

I didn't flinch. I couldn't. The team needed me to hold it together. They needed me to be the one who didn't break, no matter how much this monster tried to shake me.

The Spectator took another step forward, the darkness seeming to move with him, engulfing the park. "I've been watching you, Emma. I know everything about you—your fears, your weaknesses. It's why I've played this game. It's why I know you'll fail."

Suddenly, the moment felt too large, too overwhelming. I couldn't shake the feeling that the walls were closing in on me. I glanced around, every shadow, every corner seemed to hide something sinister. He was right. This wasn't a game anymore—it was a hunt. And I was the prey.

Before I could respond, the Spectator's hand darted toward Ryan, grabbing him by the throat. "You're not needed here anymore," he sneered, his voice low and venomous.

Ryan's struggles were futile, his legs kicking as he gasped for air. I moved instinctively, but before I could pull my gun from its holster, the Spectator flicked his wrist, and something sharp glinted in the light. A knife. Ryan's eyes widened, the terror too clear on his face.

In that moment, everything seemed to freeze. My breath caught in my throat as the Spectator pressed the blade against Ryan's neck, his eyes never leaving mine.

"Are you ready to listen, Detective?" The Spectator's voice was cold, calculating. "I have no interest in continuing this charade. You're wasting time."

I had to think. Fast. The feeling of helplessness threatened to consume me, but I pushed it down. There was no time for fear. I had one chance. One shot.

"Let him go," I ordered, my voice a tight whisper of authority. The words burned in my throat, but I forced them out.

The Spectator tilted his head, amused. "You think I'm the one who's in control here, don't you?" He pushed the blade deeper into Ryan's skin, and I heard a faint gasp escape from his lips.

I took a breath and stepped forward. Slowly, deliberately. My eyes never left the Spectator's, but my hands remained steady. "You're not going to kill him. Not while I'm standing here."

He laughed again, the sound guttural and dark. "We'll see about that."

With a sudden motion, the Spectator shoved Ryan to the ground, his body crumpling like a ragdoll. Ryan gasped, struggling to breathe, but he wasn't dead. Not yet.

"Get up!" I shouted, my heart pounding in my chest. I didn't know if Ryan had it in him, but I needed him to move.

Ryan's hands trembled as he pushed himself up, his eyes wide with fear. He was still alive, but for how long? The Spectator's games were becoming more dangerous by the minute.

I glanced quickly at my phone—there was no time left to waste. The team had to be notified. The Spectator was toying with us, but we couldn't let him win. He had already made his move. Now, it was our turn.

In the split second of distraction, I saw it—the subtle flicker of movement in the trees behind the Spectator. Someone was watching. And in the blink of an eye, I knew that the game had shifted once again. But this time, we weren't the ones calling the shots.

The hunter had become the hunted.

Chapter 14: The Meeting in the Shadows

The city was cloaked in darkness, but that didn't stop the tension from seeping through every corner of the dimly lit alley. The streets were empty, save for the occasional distant sound of traffic or the low hum of the city's electric lights. I stood at the edge of the alley, waiting for Elizabeth Blackwood. Her reputation preceded her—powerful, ruthless, and capable of playing both sides of the political and business spectrum without ever breaking a sweat. She was a woman who could destroy people as easily as she could build them up, and her connections reached deeper than most could imagine.

I was supposed to meet her here, under the cloak of night. The risks were high, but this could be the break I needed to finally understand who the Spectator was. According to our sources, Elizabeth knew something—something crucial. She had ties to many of the city's most influential figures, and if anyone could give us the answers we desperately needed, it was her.

But trusting Elizabeth Blackwood was like trusting a snake not to bite. She was known for playing a dangerous game, and I couldn't afford to let my guard down, no matter what information she had.

The sound of footsteps echoed through the alley, and I tensed. I was prepared for this moment, but that didn't make it any easier. The figure that emerged from the shadows was tall and dressed in a black coat that seemed to absorb the night around her. Her face, framed by dark, neatly styled hair, was inscrutable. Elizabeth Blackwood was just as I remembered her from the few brief encounters I'd had with her before—elegant, composed, and always in control.

"Detective Woodward," she said smoothly, her voice laced with a mixture of curiosity and amusement. She didn't offer a handshake, nor did she seem in a hurry to speak. Her eyes scanned me quickly, calculating. "I must admit, I'm surprised you decided to come alone."

"I didn't come for a social visit," I replied, keeping my voice even. "I need information. And I believe you have it."

She tilted her head, a faint smile playing at the corners of her lips. "You think I know the Spectator's identity? How flattering." Her words were tinged with sarcasm, but there was something in her expression that told me she wasn't completely dismissing the idea.

"I don't think you know. I know you do," I said, stepping closer to her. "You're playing a dangerous game, Elizabeth. If you're willing to help me, you need to understand what's at stake. Lives are on the line. But if you're playing this for your own gain, then—"

"Then you'll arrest me, or worse?" she interrupted, her tone sharp, her eyes flashing momentarily with something fierce. "Is that how you see me, Detective? A pawn in your investigation? You think I'm just a chess piece in some larger game?" She paused, her gaze becoming piercing. "You're wrong."

I didn't back down, even though her words seemed to slice through the tension between us. "What I see is a woman who knows the right people—and who's not afraid to get her hands dirty when it benefits her. You don't strike me as the type to play games you can't control."

She took a step forward, her heels clicking on the concrete, a calculated movement. "You're right. I don't play games I can't control." Her voice softened, and she leaned in just slightly, the words dripping with something more intimate, more dangerous. "But there's always a chance to bend the rules, isn't there?"

My patience was starting to thin. I had no time for her games. "Enough with the cryptic talk. What do you know about the Spectator?"

Elizabeth studied me for a moment, her face unreadable. She was deliberating—choosing her next words with care. Then, finally, she sighed, as if bored with the formality.

"The Spectator is someone who has been watching you, Emma. For months. He's been testing you, pushing your every limit. What you don't understand, Detective, is that he's not some common criminal. He's someone with power, someone who can pull strings in ways that would make your head spin. And you, you're just the next piece in his game."

I clenched my fists, feeling a pulse of anger surge through me. "This isn't a game. People are dying."

Elizabeth's gaze flickered with something faintly resembling empathy, but it was gone as quickly as it came. She shifted her stance, folding her arms across her chest as though bracing herself for what came next.

"You're right. People are dying. But not for the reasons you think." She paused again, this time letting the silence stretch between us. "The Spectator doesn't care about those people. He doesn't care about the politicians, the businessmen, or anyone else. He's out for something bigger. A message. And if you want to stop him, you need to stop looking at the victims as mere casualties of a crime."

I narrowed my eyes, trying to make sense of what she was saying. "Then what is he after?"

Elizabeth's lips curled into a small smile, one that felt more like a warning than a gesture of comfort. "You're missing the point. The Spectator is not after the people you think he is. He's targeting the ones who think they're untouchable. The ones who think they control everything. But the truth is, Detective, they don't control anything. Not anymore."

I took a deep breath, trying to steady myself, but the pieces were starting to slip through my fingers. Elizabeth was right about one thing—the Spectator wasn't just some random killer. There was a bigger plan at play, something that stretched far beyond simple murder. But how far did this conspiracy go? And who, in this city, could be trusted?

"You're still not answering my question," I pressed. "Who is he? What's his next move?"

Elizabeth took another slow step closer, and her voice dropped to a whisper, the weight of her words settling like lead in the air. "If you want the answer, you'll have to follow the money. The Spectator is connected to something much bigger than you're imagining. Politics, business—it's all intertwined. But I'm not going to give you the name you're after, Detective. I'm not that kind of person." She paused, looking me directly in the eye. "But you're close. Just a little closer, and you'll see everything. The question is—how far are you willing to go?"

I swallowed, fighting the impulse to recoil. Elizabeth's words were dangerous. She was leading me somewhere—pushing me toward a precipice I wasn't sure I was ready to face. But I had no choice. I had to follow her lead, no matter the cost.

I nodded slowly. "I'll go as far as I need to. Just give me the truth."

Elizabeth turned, her movements smooth, her coat swirling behind her. "Then keep your eyes open, Detective. The truth is closer than you think. But be careful—it might just destroy you."

As she disappeared back into the shadows, I was left standing alone, the weight of her words pressing down on me. I had been warned. Now, I had to decide whether I was ready to face the truth—whatever it might be.

Chapter 15: The Witness Who Knows Too Much

The room smelled of stale coffee and tension as Michael Thompson sat across from Emma and Thorne. His hands trembled, and his eyes darted nervously toward the door every few seconds, as if he were expecting someone to burst in at any moment. His thin, disheveled appearance told a story of sleepless nights, fear, and an overwhelming sense of paranoia. Yet despite the obvious signs of distress, he was adamant about one thing: he had seen something—something that could change everything.

"I need you to believe me," Michael said, his voice cracking as he wiped his forehead with the back of his hand. "I know what I saw, and I'm telling you, this is bigger than you think."

Emma leaned forward, studying him closely. She had seen enough witnesses to recognize when someone was genuinely scared and when they were simply trying to spin a story. Michael's anxiety wasn't just from nerves—it was palpable, raw, like he had just walked out of a nightmare and couldn't shake the images. He had been at the scene of the second murder, the one involving the prominent businessman with ties to the mayor's office. His statement had been vague before, but now, he was offering something different. Something that could finally connect the dots.

"Tell us again, Michael," Thorne said, his voice steady, almost soothing, as if trying to calm the man's fraying nerves. "You said you saw someone at the scene that night, someone who shouldn't have been there. Who was it?"

Michael looked around, lowering his voice to a near whisper. "It was him. The Spectator. I'm sure of it. I saw him standing there, watching. He was watching everything, just waiting." His eyes locked with Emma's, pleading for her to understand. "I couldn't see his face, but I know it was him. He knew I saw him. I know he did."

Emma exchanged a quick glance with Thorne. There was something about Michael's words that didn't sit right with her. On the one hand, his fear seemed real—he wasn't just repeating a rehearsed story. But on the other hand, his account seemed so far-fetched, so extreme. Could a man really have seen the Spectator that night without being caught or without the killer taking action?

"You're sure it was him?" Emma asked, her voice calm but probing. "You didn't mistake him for someone else?"

Michael shook his head violently. "No. I saw the figure. I saw the black coat, the posture. It was like he was... orchestrating everything. Like he was controlling it all. I know what I saw, and it's not just paranoia. I'm not crazy."

Thorne remained silent, his arms crossed over his chest, watching Michael intently. It was clear that he wasn't fully convinced either. Michael had been in the right place at the right time to have seen something significant, but there were so many unknowns in his story. How could the Spectator have been there and not acted? How could someone who had already killed twice leave behind a witness?

"You're telling us that the Spectator didn't do anything to stop you from seeing him?" Thorne asked, raising an eyebrow. "After everything he's done, he didn't even make an effort to silence you?"

Michael's voice dropped to a whisper, and his eyes widened with a hint of something darker. "He didn't need to. He knew I wouldn't talk. Not unless he allowed it."

Emma frowned, her mind racing. What did that mean? Michael wasn't making sense. If the Spectator was truly watching him, why hadn't he taken more direct action? And what was this about "allowing" Michael to talk?

"I don't understand," Emma said slowly, leaning forward. "You're saying he... let you go? Why?"

Michael's breath hitched, and he looked down at his hands, wringing them together nervously. "Because he wants something from me. He's not done yet. He's not done with me or with you." He looked up suddenly, his eyes wide with fear. "He's sending a message. He wants you to know that he's watching you. Every move you make."

The room was silent for a long moment as Emma and Thorne processed his words. The Spectator had always been one step ahead, always in control, always watching. Michael's testimony, though riddled with gaps, seemed to suggest something darker—that the Spectator wasn't just killing at random. He was toying with them. Or worse, manipulating them into a trap.

Emma sat back in her chair, rubbing her temples. "So, you're telling us that the Spectator is not only killing people, but he's also sending us these messages—through you?"

Michael nodded, his eyes darting around as though he expected someone to be listening in. "Yes. He's trying to make you question everything. He knows you're close to figuring it out. He wants you to doubt yourselves. To second-guess everything."

Thorne let out a long sigh. "And you expect us to believe you? You're saying that you were there, saw him, and now you're telling us that he's just been... letting you go? Just letting you talk?"

Michael's face paled, and his voice cracked again. "I know it sounds crazy, but it's the truth. I'm telling you, I saw him. He's not just some random killer. He's... controlling everything. And now, he's letting me talk, letting me tell you what I know. But I'm scared. I'm scared that if I say too much, he'll come after me. He'll come after my family."

Emma felt the weight of his words settling in. She had always known that the Spectator was methodical, that he was playing a game with them. But now, it seemed like he was stepping up his tactics—pulling the strings from the shadows, manipulating the investigation itself.

"I don't know, Michael," Emma said softly. "You're giving us a lot to think about. But your story doesn't add up. There are too many holes. Why didn't he do anything when you saw him? Why let you go?"

Michael's eyes filled with tears as he clenched his fists. "Because he wants to see how far you'll go. He wants to see if you're willing to believe me. If you're willing to stop him before it's too late."

The silence in the room was deafening. Emma's mind was racing, trying to make sense of everything Michael had said. Was he a witness telling the truth, or was he just another pawn in the Spectator's game? How could they possibly know?

Thorne stood up, his face unreadable. "We'll have to look into this more. We can't ignore what you're saying, Michael. But for now, you need to stay safe. Don't contact anyone else. We'll be in touch."

Michael nodded weakly, standing up as well, his legs trembling beneath him. As he left the room, Emma's gaze lingered on the door, her thoughts a swirl of doubt and suspicion. She wanted to believe him—she had to. But something didn't feel right. The pieces weren't fitting together.

She turned to Thorne, her voice low. "Do you think he's telling the truth?"

Thorne didn't answer immediately. He just stared at the door where Michael had left, his brow furrowed in thought. Finally, he spoke.

"I don't know, Emma. But if he is... we might just be playing into the Spectator's hands."

Chapter 16: The Silent Crusade

The investigation had reached a turning point. Emma sat at her desk, surrounded by piles of case files, photographs, and maps that had accumulated over the last several weeks. Her mind felt clouded as she sifted through the information again and again, trying to connect the dots. Something had shifted in the way she was viewing the Spectator, the killer who had haunted their every step, always lurking in the background, pulling the strings with an unseen hand.

It was becoming clearer now that this wasn't just a spree of random murders. No, the Spectator was targeting more than individuals; he was sending a message, trying to reshape the very fabric of the system. Emma had sensed it before, but now the pieces fit together with a chilling sense of inevitability. This wasn't about personal vendettas or fleeting moments of rage. The Spectator was on a crusade.

"We've been looking at this all wrong," Emma muttered to herself as she reviewed the notes once more. She felt a shift in her understanding of the killer's motives. What if the Spectator wasn't just punishing individuals for personal wrongs? What if these killings were part of a larger agenda, a mission to cleanse the city of its perceived corruption? It was an idea that had been growing in her mind over the past few days, ever since Michael Thompson had come forward with his account of seeing the killer at the second crime scene.

Emma's thoughts were interrupted when Thorne walked into the room, his face weary but determined. He had been busy tracking down leads, following up on witnesses, and trying to piece together the fragmented trail the Spectator had left behind. They had made some progress, but the killer always seemed to stay a step ahead.

"You're thinking about the Spectator again," Thorne said, his voice low but understanding. He knew the investigation was taking its toll on Emma, just as it had on him.

Emma nodded without looking up. "I don't think this is just about personal revenge anymore. It's more than that. I think he sees himself as some sort of crusader, trying to purge the city of its rot. Each victim isn't just an individual—it's a symbol of everything wrong with the system."

Thorne was silent for a moment, processing her words. He walked over to the board where they had pinned up pictures of the victims, notes, and connections. The string of murders had seemed like isolated events at first, each tied to a different part of the city's political and business landscape. But now, as Emma had pointed out, a deeper pattern was emerging. There was something methodical in the way each victim had been chosen. They weren't just random people—they were influential figures, connected to corruption, greed, and power.

"I've been looking at the backgrounds of each of these victims," Thorne said, pointing to the photos on the wall. "The businessman, the judge, the high-ranking police officer. They all had something to do with the darker side of the system. The mayor's office, corporate deals, backroom politics. It's like he's targeting the very heart of the corruption."

"Exactly," Emma replied, feeling a sense of urgency rising in her chest. "He's not just taking lives; he's taking down the structures that prop up the system. He's sending a message that the entire foundation is broken, and he's doing whatever it takes to bring it down, one piece at a time."

Thorne nodded grimly. "It's almost like he believes he's saving the city. Purging it of the people who hold too much power and control."

Emma's eyes narrowed as she stared at the photos again, seeing them in a new light. Each one of the victims had been a symbol of influence in some way. A businessman with ties to the mayor's office, a judge known for his harsh rulings on corruption, a police officer involved in high-level cover-ups. They were all connected to the power structures that governed the city—structures the Spectator seemed determined to dismantle.

"The more I think about it," Emma continued, "the more it makes sense. He's a vigilante—only, he's not just punishing people. He's trying to expose something much bigger, something systemic. He wants to break the system down from within, using violence to show the city what's really happening behind the closed doors of power."

Thorne looked at her with a mixture of concern and disbelief. "So, you think he sees himself as some kind of... hero? A soldier in a crusade against corruption?"

Emma met his gaze, her expression hardening. "Yes, I do. And that's what makes him so dangerous. He's not acting out of emotion or personal hatred.

He's acting out of a twisted sense of justice. He believes that by killing these people, he's saving the city from itself."

Thorne crossed his arms, his jaw tightening as he absorbed the weight of her words. He had always known that the Spectator was calculating, but he hadn't considered the possibility that the killer saw himself as a force for good. "If that's true, then we're not just dealing with a killer. We're dealing with someone who believes they're on a mission. Someone who's not going to stop until they think they've completed it."

Emma stood up abruptly, her mind racing. "We need to figure out what his next move is. We need to stop him before he kills again. But more than that, we need to understand where he's coming from. If we can understand his motive, we can predict his next target."

Thorne's expression softened. "I'll get in touch with our contacts. We need to find out if there's anyone else with a similar pattern of behavior—someone who could have influenced him, or someone he's following."

Emma nodded, the weight of the investigation settling heavily on her shoulders. The deeper they dug, the more she realized that this wasn't just about catching a killer. This was about stopping a force that believed it was acting for the greater good, no matter the cost. The Spectator wasn't just a criminal. He was a symbol of everything wrong with the system—and he was using murder as his weapon.

As Thorne left to follow up on his leads, Emma stood by the window, staring out at the city below. The dark, sprawling metropolis seemed so distant, so detached from the realities of the investigation. But Emma knew the truth now. The Spectator wasn't just attacking individuals—he was attacking the very soul of the city. And until they stopped him, the crusade would continue, one victim at a time.

Emma's phone buzzed on her desk, pulling her from her thoughts. She glanced at the screen. A new message from Natalie Sinclair, their cyber-crime expert. The subject read: "The Spectator's Digital Footprint—A Lead." Emma's heart quickened. Could this be the break they were waiting for?

She grabbed the phone and began reading the message, her mind already racing with possibilities. This could be the clue that would finally lead them to the Spectator.

Chapter 17: The Deal with the Devil

The tension in Emma's gut had been building for days, and it hadn't subsided since the moment she received the message. Elizabeth Blackwood—the woman with connections so deep that they ran through the very veins of the city's power structure—was waiting for her. Emma had known it was coming. She had felt the growing pressure, the pull toward the inevitable. Elizabeth's name had been circling like a shadow, and Emma couldn't ignore it any longer. She needed information—information that only Elizabeth could provide.

But Emma was no fool. She knew the price of dealing with someone like Elizabeth. The woman was a master manipulator, a puppet master who could twist anything to her advantage. Trusting her could be disastrous, but without Elizabeth's knowledge, the case would stall. Emma had reached a point where she had no other options.

Sitting in her car outside the hotel where Elizabeth had asked to meet, Emma's hands gripped the steering wheel. The city was buzzing with activity all around her, but in that moment, it felt eerily quiet. The weight of the decision pressed down on her, making the air feel thick. If she went in, she would have to accept that there was no going back. Once she made the deal, she would be bound by it—whether she liked it or not.

Elizabeth had promised her information that could bring the investigation closer to an end. The Spectator's true identity, she claimed, was within Emma's reach. But in exchange for that knowledge, Elizabeth demanded a favor—a favor that Emma had no desire to fulfill. The specifics had been vague, but Emma knew that whatever it was, it would force her to compromise her own values.

Taking a deep breath, Emma pushed open the car door and stepped out, the cold night air hitting her face. The hotel loomed ahead, its glass windows reflecting the city lights in distorted patterns. It seemed too pristine, too perfect for what was about to unfold inside.

As Emma walked into the lobby, she kept her posture straight, her face unreadable. She couldn't afford to show any sign of weakness. She had been in situations like this before—dealing with criminals, manipulators, people who thrived on control. But something about Elizabeth felt different. It wasn't just her power. It was the way she carried herself, always one step ahead, always playing a game with higher stakes.

Emma was led to a private room in the back, where Elizabeth was already waiting. The woman sat behind a sleek black desk, her presence commanding the space. She was dressed in a tailored suit, her dark hair perfectly styled, her makeup flawless. Everything about her radiated control, as if she could bend the world to her will with a single word.

"Detective Knight," Elizabeth said with a smile that didn't quite reach her eyes. "I'm glad you could make it."

Emma didn't respond immediately, her gaze flickering over the room. There was a sense of heaviness here, an undercurrent of something dangerous. She could almost feel the weight of the walls closing in. She took a seat across from Elizabeth, keeping her back straight, her fingers tapping lightly on the armrest.

"I'm here, Elizabeth," Emma said, her voice steady, though inside, her thoughts were running in overdrive. "I need the information you promised. I'm not here to play games."

Elizabeth's lips curled into a smile, a predatory gleam in her eyes. "Of course. I wouldn't dream of wasting your time." She paused, letting the silence stretch between them for a moment before leaning forward. "But you understand, Detective, that everything comes with a price."

Emma's pulse quickened, but she kept her face impassive. "What do you want?"

"Oh, nothing too complicated," Elizabeth said with a casual wave of her hand. "A simple favor, really. Something that will require you to... bend the rules, just a little. But don't worry, it'll be well worth your while. You'll see."

Emma's mind raced as she weighed her options. She had known from the start that Elizabeth wouldn't just hand over the information without asking for something in return. What bothered her, however, was the vague nature of the request. Elizabeth had given no specifics, only a promise that Emma would find it "worthwhile." That was the most unsettling part. Elizabeth had the power to make even the smallest favors feel like monumental obligations.

"You've got my attention," Emma said, trying to keep her tone neutral. "What do you need?"

Elizabeth's smile deepened. "It's simple. I need you to use your position to influence the outcome of a certain investigation. There's a case that's...

troublesome for me, Detective. It involves one of my associates, someone I can't afford to see go down. You understand, don't you?"

Emma felt a chill run down her spine. The implication was clear—Elizabeth wanted her to compromise the integrity of her work, to use her authority to protect someone who likely didn't deserve it. The thought made her stomach turn. It wasn't just a matter of bending the rules; it was about breaking them entirely.

"You want me to cover up a crime," Emma said, her voice icy. "That's not something I can do."

Elizabeth didn't flinch. "It's not about covering anything up, Emma. It's about ensuring that justice is served in the right way. You and I both know that sometimes, the law isn't the answer. Sometimes, the system needs to be... reformed." She leaned forward, her eyes locking onto Emma's. "And you're in a perfect position to make that happen."

Emma stared at her, feeling a storm of conflicting emotions churn within her. This wasn't just about getting information anymore. This was a test of her character, of everything she had stood for. Elizabeth was asking her to make a choice between integrity and power—between doing what was right and doing what was convenient.

She knew she couldn't trust Elizabeth, but she also knew that without this deal, they would have no way of catching the Spectator. It was the kind of choice that could haunt her for the rest of her career—and her life.

"I'll think about it," Emma said finally, her voice low.

Elizabeth's smile widened, but her eyes remained sharp. "Of course. Take your time, Detective. But remember, the clock is ticking. Information doesn't wait forever."

Emma stood up, her mind a whirlwind of thoughts. As she walked toward the door, Elizabeth's voice followed her.

"Don't take too long," Elizabeth called out. "The deal won't be on the table forever."

As Emma stepped out of the room, she felt the weight of the decision pressing down on her. This was no longer just about the Spectator—it was about the path she would choose to walk. And the consequences of that choice would echo far beyond this investigation.

Chapter 18: The Web of Lies

The investigation had taken a turn neither Emma nor her team had expected. For months, they had been chasing the Spectator's trail through a maze of cryptic messages, dead ends, and false leads. But now, the pieces were starting to fall into place, and the bigger picture was emerging—a picture far darker than they had anticipated.

Emma stood over the large map spread across the conference room table, her fingers tracing the connections between the victims. What had initially appeared to be random acts of violence tied to personal vendettas was now starting to look like something much more coordinated. Each of the victims had been a key player in a larger game, and their deaths seemed less like a series of isolated murders and more like a deliberate attempt to shake the foundations of the city's power structure.

It wasn't just about revenge. The Spectator was sending a message—one that was slowly revealing itself to be a far-reaching conspiracy.

"We've been looking at this all wrong," Emma muttered, mostly to herself, as she scanned the map once more.

Thorne, who had been studying the board beside her, looked up. "What do you mean?"

"The killings—they're not random. The Spectator's targeting people who are connected, people with power," Emma said, her voice heavy with realization. "And they're all connected to something bigger—something we've been missing."

Thorne's brow furrowed as he glanced over the list of names and connections pinned to the wall. "You think it's a conspiracy?"

Emma's eyes narrowed. "I don't think it. I know it."

The team had been gathering intelligence on the Spectator for weeks now, piecing together everything from business ties to political affiliations, and the more they dug, the more alarming the connections became. At first, the victims seemed like outliers—men and women with questionable ethics, involved in scandals, known to walk the line of corruption. But as they continued to investigate, it became clear that these weren't just isolated bad apples.

The victims were part of a much larger web—a web that spanned across government, law enforcement, and business. Powerful figures who, on the surface, appeared to have nothing in common were all linked through a network of shady deals, backroom politics, and unspoken alliances. And at the center of this web, Emma now realized, was something even more sinister: the Spectator.

"I don't get it," Thorne said, running a hand through his hair. "Why target these people? What does the Spectator hope to accomplish?"

Emma's eyes shifted to the list of names. Some of them were business tycoons, others were government officials, and a few were high-ranking law enforcement officers. All of them had been complicit in corruption, but some were much more deeply involved than others. She thought about it for a moment before answering.

"The Spectator sees themselves as a crusader," Emma said, her voice filled with a mixture of disgust and understanding. "They think they're cleaning up the city. Purging it of corruption."

Thorne's face twisted with confusion. "By killing people?"

Emma nodded grimly. "Yes. They believe that the only way to save this city is to eliminate the ones who are corrupting it. And the deeper we dig, the more we realize that this corruption runs all the way to the top."

The team had uncovered more than just the names of the victims. They had begun to dig into the financial records, phone records, and personal connections of the people the Spectator had targeted. And what they found was shocking.

One of the first victims, a wealthy businessman with ties to the mayor's office, had been involved in laundering money for organized crime syndicates. Another victim, a judge who had been known for his strict rulings on corruption cases, had been taking bribes from a notorious crime family for years. The connections between the victims ran so deep that Emma felt as though they were unraveling an entire underworld that had been hiding in plain sight.

"Are we even sure who we're looking for anymore?" Thorne asked. "It's like the Spectator is just a symbol, and there's no one person behind it."

Emma didn't respond immediately. She had been wrestling with that very question. For a long time, they had thought the Spectator was one person—a lone figure acting as judge, jury, and executioner. But now, she wasn't so sure. The pattern of killings was too intricate, too well thought out. This didn't feel like the work of a single individual; it felt like a much larger operation, a collective effort by those who had been hiding in the shadows for years.

"It could be one person," Emma said slowly, her mind churning with possibilities. "But it could also be a group. A network of people, all working together to bring down the system."

Thorne seemed to consider this for a moment. "A group, huh? That would explain the planning. The Spectator's actions are calculated—almost surgical. And if there are more people involved, they could be using this campaign to tear down the city's entire infrastructure, one leader at a time."

Emma nodded, her eyes narrowing as she thought about the implications. If there was a network of people involved in these killings, it would mean that the conspiracy reached farther than anyone had imagined. It would mean that the Spectator's actions were just the beginning. The true conspiracy—whatever it was—could bring the entire city to its knees.

"We need to be careful," Emma said, her voice quiet but urgent. "If we expose this, we risk bringing down more than just a few criminals. We'll be exposing the entire system—politicians, businessmen, law enforcement. It's a powder keg waiting to explode."

Thorne's face tightened, and he took a deep breath. "So what's the next step?"

Emma exhaled slowly. "We keep digging. But we need to be strategic. We can't go in guns blazing. If we blow the lid off this thing too early, we risk destabilizing everything. We need proof—solid, irrefutable proof—before we make our move."

The room fell into a heavy silence as Emma glanced at the others. They had come so far, but now they stood on the edge of something far more dangerous. This wasn't just a murder case anymore; it was a ticking time bomb, one that threatened to take down everyone involved—her, the team, the entire city.

But Emma knew there was no turning back. They were in too deep now. And whatever happened next, she had no choice but to follow the trail to its bitter end.

"Let's get to work," Emma said finally, her voice steady and determined. "The truth is out there. And it's time we brought it to light."

Chapter 19: The Shadow of Betrayal

The day started like any other—busy, chaotic, and filled with the relentless pursuit of answers. Emma had long ago grown accustomed to the weight of the investigation, but today felt different. There was a tension in the air, a subtle shift that she couldn't quite put her finger on. She chalked it up to the pressure mounting from all sides—deadlines closing in, the Spectator's next move looming, and the political machine grinding on in the background, seemingly oblivious to the storm gathering in its midst.

The team gathered for their usual morning briefing in the conference room. The air was thick with quiet urgency as everyone filed in, taking their places around the large table. But something was off. Emma couldn't shake the feeling that someone was hiding something. The subtle glances exchanged between her team members, the way they avoided her eyes, it all made her skin crawl.

"Alright, everyone," Emma began, trying to push the unease to the back of her mind. "Let's go over what we've got. We're closing in on the Spectator. We need to stay focused."

She began outlining their progress, highlighting key leads, and making sure everyone was on the same page. As she spoke, her eyes drifted over to Thorne, who was scribbling notes, his expression tight. He looked like he had something on his mind, but when he met her gaze, he quickly looked away. Emma noticed it but didn't call attention to it. They had too much to deal with.

When the briefing ended, Emma dismissed everyone with a brief nod. But as she turned to leave the room, her phone buzzed. It was a text message, one from an anonymous number.

I know what you're planning. You can't trust anyone.

Emma's heart skipped a beat as she read the words. The message sent a chill down her spine. It wasn't a warning; it was a threat. And the timing couldn't have been worse. For the first time in months, she felt the weight of the investigation pushing back against her. Something was wrong. But who would be behind this?

She quickly scanned the room. Her team members were all gathered in small groups, talking among themselves, unaware of her growing alarm. But the message had unsettled her—deeply. She had trusted everyone around her. Or at least, she had thought she did.

Emma left the room, her mind racing. She needed answers. She couldn't let this slide, not when they were so close to the truth. She pulled her phone out again and checked the number. No name. No clue. Just a series of digits that led nowhere. A dead end.

She paced for a moment, trying to regain her focus. The investigation had already put enough strain on her relationships, on her ability to trust anyone. Now, this. Someone within the team was playing both sides. Someone had betrayed her. But who?

Her first instinct was to confront Thorne. He had been the one who had looked away, acting distant during the briefing. Had he been the one to send the message? It was a possibility, but it didn't make sense. Thorne had been by her side for too long. She trusted him. He had never given her a reason to doubt him. But now... now, everything seemed uncertain.

Before she could make up her mind, her phone buzzed again. This time, it was a voicemail. The voice on the other end was distorted, a deep, garbled tone that made it almost impossible to understand. But as she played the message back a second time, one phrase came through clearly.

"You're being watched."

Emma felt the blood drain from her face. It was as though the walls were closing in on her. Someone was watching them—watching her. Whoever this was, they knew too much. They knew the investigation, they knew her team, and they knew what steps they were taking next. The Spectator had to be involved somehow. But the thought that someone close to her could be playing both sides... that thought was unbearable.

"Emma?"

She turned quickly to find Thorne standing in the doorway of the hallway, his face drawn with concern. He must have noticed her tension. The look in his eyes said everything she needed to know. He was worried. But what was he worried about?

"Are you okay?" Thorne asked, his voice low.

"I need to talk to you," Emma said, her voice barely above a whisper. "Now."

They walked briskly to her office, and as soon as the door closed behind them, Emma fixed her eyes on him. She wasn't going to beat around the bush. She couldn't afford to.

"Thorne," she began, her voice steady but with a bite to it, "someone sent me a message today. A warning. They said I can't trust anyone. And now, I'm wondering if I can trust you."

Thorne's eyes widened, a flash of surprise crossing his face before he quickly masked it. "Emma, what are you talking about?"

"I'm talking about a betrayal," Emma said, her voice tight with a mixture of anger and disbelief. "Someone on the team is working against us. I don't know who, but they've been feeding information to the Spectator. They know everything we're planning. They're watching us."

Thorne took a step back, his hand gripping the back of a chair for support. "What makes you think it's one of us?" he asked, his voice strained.

"Because the Spectator knew about our moves. The information was too precise. Too accurate. They know exactly where we're headed next. Someone on this team has been feeding them information," Emma said, her tone hard. "And I need to know who."

There was a long, pregnant silence before Thorne spoke again. "Emma, you've known me for years. I've been with you through everything. You really think I'd betray you?"

Emma shook her head slowly, her mind still reeling. "I don't know who I can trust anymore. I can't shake the feeling that someone is playing both sides. I don't know if it's you, or Ryan, or Natalie, or even—" she stopped herself, her heart sinking. "I don't know."

Thorne stepped forward then, his face softening with a mix of concern and guilt. "Emma, listen to me. I'm not the one doing this. I swear to you."

But Emma's eyes were distant, filled with doubt. She wanted to believe him, she really did. But the message—the call, the cryptic warning—had shaken her to her core. And in the dark corner of her mind, the seed of doubt had been planted. Could she truly trust him? Or had the killer been one step ahead, manipulating them all from the inside?

"Who else could it be?" Emma murmured, her voice almost to herself.

Thorne's expression hardened. "I don't know. But we need to find out. Fast."

For a brief moment, Emma thought she saw something in his eyes—something that made her stomach churn. Fear, perhaps. Or maybe something more dangerous. She wasn't sure. But she had no time to dwell on it. They were running out of time, and the shadow of betrayal loomed large over them all.

"Let's get to work," Emma said, her voice sharp. "We're not backing down. But trust… that's something I'm not sure I have right now."

Chapter 20: The Pursuit of Justice

The clock was ticking. Every second felt like a hammer against Emma's chest, each one bringing them closer to the next murder, the next victim. The team had pushed themselves to the limit, sifting through countless pieces of evidence, chasing down leads, but with each step forward, it felt like they were two steps behind. The Spectator was always one move ahead, leaving no trace, no sign. The killer's precision had been chilling from the start, and as they neared their breaking point, the pressure only intensified.

"We don't have much time," Emma said, standing before the board filled with photographs and notes, all of them pointing to one thing: the killer's final target. They had narrowed it down to a handful of possible candidates, each one with ties to the political elite, each one an easy target for the Spectator's twisted sense of justice.

Thorne stood across from her, his arms crossed, his face drawn. "We know who they're going after next. The question is, how do we stop it?"

Emma sighed, rubbing her eyes. The weight of the investigation, of the mounting casualties, of the broken trust among her own team, was starting to crush her. The emotional toll had become unbearable. But she couldn't afford to give in to it. Not now. Not when they were so close.

"We've traced their movements, their patterns," Emma said, voice steady despite the exhaustion. "We've narrowed it down to one of three targets. We know the Spectator likes to strike when they think the victim is most vulnerable. They'll be in a place where they feel safe. A place they trust."

Thorne nodded. "And we have to be ready to stop them before that happens."

"I know," Emma said, her gaze hardening. "But I need you to understand something. This isn't just about stopping a killer anymore. This is about bringing justice to a city that has been broken, to a system that has failed everyone."

Her words hung in the air, heavy with meaning. She wasn't just talking about the Spectator anymore. She was talking about the city itself, the corruption that ran through every level of power, the system that allowed these murders to happen in the first place. The Spectator might be the face of the reckoning, but Emma knew the true fight was much larger than one killer. It was about exposing everything—every lie, every betrayal, every rotten piece of the system.

"I know," Thorne said quietly. "We're all in this together. We won't let the killer get away. But we need to be careful. If we make one wrong move, we could lose everything."

Emma met his eyes, her determination unwavering. "We don't have the luxury of waiting. We'll take our chances, and we'll do it right this time."

They had no choice. The Spectator was closing in on the final target. Emma had spent the last twenty-four hours preparing the team, working with the intelligence they had gathered, trying to predict the killer's next move. But even with all their resources, they still didn't know for sure where the attack would take place. Time was running out, and she had to make the call.

"We need to split up," Emma said, her voice sharper now, decisive. "Thorne, take Natalie and Ryan. You go to the last known address of the victim's family, make sure they're secure. Get them out of there if you need to. I'll stay here and coordinate with the rest of the team. We'll monitor everything we can, and if the Spectator makes a move, we'll stop it before they strike."

Thorne hesitated, a flicker of doubt crossing his face. "Are you sure? You're not going alone, Emma."

She could see the concern in his eyes, and for a moment, she almost let herself give in to it. But she couldn't. She had to do this. Alone.

"I'm not going alone," Emma said firmly. "I've got backup here. You just focus on your part."

Thorne opened his mouth to argue, but Emma cut him off with a sharp look. "Do it. No questions. This is the only shot we've got."

Thorne met her gaze for a moment longer, his eyes searching hers, before nodding. "Alright. We'll move out in fifteen minutes. Be careful, Emma."

As Thorne and the others moved to execute their part of the plan, Emma stood at the center of the room, her mind racing. Every decision she made felt like it could be the one that either saved a life or condemned another. She could feel the weight of it—the lives that hung in the balance, the guilt that gnawed at her for every second they were behind the killer.

The room was silent now, save for the hum of computers and the soft clattering of keyboards as her team worked to track every lead. Emma's eyes darted over the wall of evidence, her mind flipping through the puzzle pieces, trying to find the one they'd missed. There had to be something—some small detail they'd overlooked. Some connection that would bring everything together.

Her phone buzzed. It was a message from an unknown number. Her heart skipped a beat as she read it.

It's happening now. You're too late.

The message sent a wave of panic through her, but she quickly pushed it aside. She couldn't afford to lose focus now. If the Spectator was already making a move, she needed to act immediately.

"Everyone!" Emma called, her voice cutting through the tense silence. "We need to mobilize now. The Spectator is on the move. It's happening right now."

The team sprang into action. Within seconds, they were all on their feet, gathering their things and heading for the door. Emma felt her pulse quicken, the adrenaline flooding her system as they raced to prevent the inevitable. She had no idea where the Spectator would strike first, but she knew one thing for sure: she wasn't going to let this killer walk away.

She grabbed her coat and headed out into the cold, the weight of the city pressing down on her. The streets were eerily quiet as they sped through the darkened alleys and neon-lit avenues. The specter of the Spectator seemed to loom over everything, a presence that couldn't be ignored.

As the team approached the target location, Emma's phone buzzed again. This time, it wasn't a message. It was a call. She answered it without hesitation.

"Emma," a voice said, barely above a whisper. "You're too late."

Her stomach dropped. She knew that voice. It was Elizabeth Blackwood.

"You don't know what you're dealing with," Elizabeth continued, her voice dripping with malice. "You think you're saving the city, but all you're doing is playing into the Spectator's hands. The game's already been won. It's too late to stop it."

Emma's heart pounded in her chest. "What do you mean? Where are they?"

Elizabeth didn't answer. The line went dead.

Emma cursed under her breath. The game had changed again. The killer had made their move, and now it was up to Emma and her team to stop the madness before it consumed them all.

Chapter 21: The Last Clue

The atmosphere in the room was thick with anticipation. The team had gathered around the table, staring at the small piece of paper they had found at the scene. It was a cryptic note, but it was the first real lead they had gotten in days. The killer had always been steps ahead, leaving nothing but shadows in their wake. But now, finally, there was something tangible—a clue that might lead them directly to the Spectator.

Emma stared at the note, trying to make sense of it. It was written in a mixture of symbols and words, some of them familiar, others entirely new. The message wasn't just a string of random letters; it felt deliberate, calculated. It was meant to be deciphered, to be unraveled. But how?

"We need to figure this out," Emma said, her voice tight. She knew the clock was ticking. The Spectator had already claimed so many lives, and with each passing minute, they were closer to the final target.

Natalie Sinclair, the cyber-crime expert, was the first to speak up. She had been studying the symbols on the note, her fingers hovering over her laptop keyboard. "Some of these symbols are similar to encryption patterns I've seen before," she said, her eyes scanning the screen as she worked. "But there's something off about it. It's not just a simple code."

Ryan Fitzgerald, the former informant, leaned over the table, his eyes narrowing. "It's a puzzle. A test. The Spectator wants us to work for it. They're playing a game with us."

Emma nodded, frustration creeping in. "That's all they've been doing—playing games. But this... this could be our chance. We need to crack it now."

They all turned their attention to the screen as Natalie typed rapidly, trying various decryption methods. The symbols shifted on the screen, but nothing seemed to work. She paused, her fingers hovering over the keys, as though waiting for some kind of breakthrough. The tension in the room was unbearable.

"This... this is different," she muttered, finally pressing a key. The symbols shifted again, and this time, a string of letters appeared—something that resembled a name.

"It's a name," Emma said, leaning forward. "What does it mean?"

Natalie scanned the screen, her eyes growing wide. "It's not just a name... it's an address. And it's connected to someone very high up."

Emma's heart skipped a beat. "Who?"

Natalie hesitated. "It's linked to a former mayor. A man named Jonathan Halloran."

The name struck Emma like a blow to the chest. Jonathan Halloran. She had heard of him, of course. Everyone in the city had. He had been a beloved mayor years ago, known for his promises to clean up the city and root out corruption. But after his sudden resignation, his name had become something of a ghost—mentioned only in passing, with rumors swirling about his alleged involvement in shady deals. No one had ever been able to prove anything. He had slipped out of the public eye, disappearing into the shadows.

But now, it seemed, the Spectator was dragging his name back into the light.

"This can't be a coincidence," Emma said, her mind racing. "Halloran was one of the most powerful men in the city. If the Spectator is targeting him, then it means—"

"Everything we've been working on," Ryan interrupted, "is connected to him. The Spectator's crusade isn't just about cleansing the city of criminals. It's about exposing the truth about everyone involved, even the ones who thought they were untouchable."

Emma clenched her fists. "We have to move fast. If Halloran is really involved, then we're dealing with more than just one killer. This could be the tip of the iceberg."

Thorne, who had been quiet up until now, spoke up. "We need to find Halloran. Now. Before the Spectator does."

"I'll call the office," Emma said, reaching for her phone. "I'll have them trace his last known location. We'll move in fast, get him to safety before anything happens."

But just as she was about to dial, the phone buzzed in her hand, and her heart skipped a beat. The message on the screen was simple, but it made her blood run cold.

"You're getting closer. But you'll never catch me."

Emma's breath caught in her throat. The Spectator was watching them. They knew they were getting close, and they weren't about to let them get away with it.

She slammed her fist on the table. "Damn it. This ends now."

The team sprang into action. The clock was ticking, and Emma could feel the weight of the moment settling on her. This was it. The final confrontation. They had the clue, they had the lead, and now they had to move quickly. No more mistakes. No more false leads. They had to find Halloran, and they had to find him fast.

Emma turned to Thorne. "You and Ryan head to the address. See what you can find. Natalie, keep working on the code. We need to know everything about Halloran—his connections, his movements, anything that could tie him to the Spectator."

As they began to move out, Emma's mind raced. If the Spectator was really going after Halloran, it meant they were about to uncover something huge—something that could bring down the entire city. Emma had never felt so close to the truth, but at the same time, she knew how dangerous this was. The closer they got, the more dangerous the situation became. Whoever was behind the Spectator was willing to go to any lengths to keep their secrets buried.

They arrived at the address in less than twenty minutes, their tires screeching to a halt in front of an old warehouse on the outskirts of the city. The place was abandoned, but there were signs that someone had been there recently. Emma felt a chill crawl up her spine as they approached the entrance.

"This is it," Thorne said, his voice grim. "Whatever happens, we need to be ready."

Emma nodded, drawing in a deep breath. They had no idea what awaited them inside, but they couldn't turn back now. They had to finish this. For the victims, for the city, for everything they had worked for.

As they stepped through the door, the silence was deafening. The only sound was the echo of their footsteps on the concrete floor. Emma's senses were on high alert, every nerve in her body screaming that something was wrong.

Suddenly, the door slammed shut behind them.

The trap had been set.

Chapter 22: Into the Lion's Den

Emma took a steadying breath as she looked over her team. They were gathered in the dimly lit briefing room, each face marked with the strain of the past few months. This would be the final push, the last attempt to bring the Spectator's reign of terror to an end. They had been tracking him for what felt like an eternity, wading through a mire of lies and half-truths, stumbling from one dark secret to another. But now, they were close—so close that she could feel the tension in the air, a buzzing anticipation that crackled like static electricity.

Natalie leaned over her laptop, typing furiously, analyzing the recent data they had pulled from Jonathan Halloran's encrypted files. After weeks of evading capture, it appeared that the Spectator was finally slipping up, leaving a trail that could lead them directly to him. But Emma knew better than to assume anything. Every clue he left, every piece of evidence, could be part of a larger plan—a deadly game designed to lure them into the lion's den.

"Here," Natalie said, breaking the silence, "I've tracked his last known movements to an abandoned building in the industrial district. It's heavily fortified, more than any ordinary warehouse would need. Cameras on every corner, but all linked to private servers. He's been operating out of there for at least the past month."

Emma looked at the coordinates on the screen. It was a bleak part of the city, a ghostly expanse of empty factories and warehouses long abandoned by their owners, swallowed by years of neglect and corruption. No one would hear them there. No one would even notice.

Thorne crossed his arms, his expression dark. "If this is his stronghold, he'll have it set up with traps and defenses. He knows we're coming."

Emma nodded, her mind racing. The Spectator was clever, calculating, and unyielding. Every step of this investigation had revealed not just a killer but a strategist—a mind fixated on exposing the city's corruption, willing to cross any line to make his twisted point. But she couldn't allow herself to be shaken by his taunts, by his threats. He thrived on fear and intimidation; the only way to defeat him was to push past the terror, to face him head-on.

Ryan Fitzgerald, the former informant who had been a reluctant ally, looked uneasy. "You sure about this, Emma? I've seen places like this before. If he knows we're coming, he'll be prepared. It won't be pretty."

Emma met his gaze. "It's now or never. If we don't take this chance, he'll slip away again, and the next victim won't just be a faceless name. He's working his way up, escalating his message. Every person he targets, every so-called 'corrupt' individual... it's all leading somewhere. If we don't stop him now, he'll take the whole city down with him."

Silence fell as they each processed the gravity of her words. The Spectator wasn't just targeting individuals; he was orchestrating a systematic assault on the city's very structure. His message was gaining traction, his name whispered in dark corners, sparking fear and admiration in equal measure. The line between vigilante and terrorist had been crossed, but in the shadows, his supporters multiplied.

Emma cleared her throat. "Everyone, gather your gear. We're going in tonight."

They moved in silence, gathering equipment, checking weapons, testing communication devices. The somber air was thick with an unspoken understanding. This was it. The final push, the last battle. They had to end it here, for better or worse.

The journey to the industrial district was quiet, each person lost in their thoughts. As they approached the coordinates Natalie had pinpointed, the building loomed ahead, a hulking mass of decayed steel and concrete, surrounded by a labyrinth of chain-link fences and barbed wire. Emma's heartbeat quickened as they parked the vehicles a safe distance away, their figures blending into the night as they moved in formation, weapons drawn.

Thorne took point, moving carefully, signaling for the others to follow. The closer they got to the entrance, the more Emma could feel the weight of unseen eyes on them, watching, waiting. She could sense the Spectator's presence, a malevolent force hovering over them, waiting for them to make the first move.

Inside, the building was eerily silent, shadows stretching across the floor, broken only by the faint glow of their flashlights. Emma scanned the room, every nerve alert, searching for signs of movement, of traps, of anything that might betray their quarry's position. They advanced through the corridors, each turn bringing them closer to the heart of the building, the place where the Spectator was most likely to be hiding.

Suddenly, a faint click echoed through the silence, followed by the unmistakable hum of machinery. Emma's instincts kicked in as she signaled for everyone to stop. But it was too late. The walls around them began to shift, heavy metal barriers sliding into place, cutting off their path and locking them inside.

"Damn it," Thorne muttered, slamming his fist against the nearest barrier. "He's trapped us."

Ryan's eyes darted around, panic flashing across his face. "This was a setup. He knew we'd come here."

Emma felt a surge of anger, a burning frustration that had been building for weeks. "Stay calm," she said, her voice steady. "This isn't over yet. There has to be a way out."

Natalie was already working, her fingers flying over her portable tablet as she attempted to hack into the building's security system. "I'm trying to override the locks, but it's… it's different than anything I've seen before. It's almost like he's guiding me."

"Guiding you?" Emma's brow furrowed.

"Yeah," Natalie said, her eyes fixed on the screen. "The encryption, the way the system is responding… it's like he wants us to go a certain direction."

Emma exchanged a look with Thorne. "It's a game to him. He wants us to follow his lead, to go where he wants us to go."

Thorne gritted his teeth. "Then we have to be careful. He's leading us into a trap, but if we don't follow, we'll be stuck in here."

Emma nodded, steeling herself. "We don't have a choice. Let's keep moving."

They followed the route the Spectator seemed to have laid out, weaving through the labyrinthine corridors, every corner a potential ambush, every step a reminder of the danger they were in. The building seemed to breathe around them, the hum of hidden machinery, the faint echoes of their footsteps reverberating through the darkness.

Finally, they reached a large chamber, a central hub with walls lined with monitors. Each screen showed a different angle of the city, images of crowded streets, government buildings, the offices of the very people the Spectator had marked as corrupt. In the center of the room stood a single chair, facing away from them, silhouetted against the glow of the screens.

Emma's heart pounded as she raised her weapon, signaling for the others to fan out. Slowly, she approached the chair, her finger hovering over the trigger. But as she drew closer, she realized with a sinking feeling that the chair was empty.

Suddenly, the monitors flickered, and a familiar voice filled the room, echoing off the walls.

"Welcome, Detective Sinclair."

Emma's blood ran cold. It was the Spectator's voice, calm and detached, as if he had been expecting them all along.

"You've come so far," the voice continued, laced with a sinister edge. "But this is only the beginning. The city is rotting from within, and you're just a pawn in a game much larger than you could ever understand."

Emma clenched her fists, resisting the urge to shout back. She wouldn't give him the satisfaction.

"You can't stop what's coming," the voice taunted. "The truth will come out, one way or another. And when it does, the city will burn."

The monitors went dark, leaving them in silence.

Emma turned to her team, her jaw set, her eyes blazing with determination. "We're getting out of here," she said, her voice unwavering. "And we're taking him down."

Chapter 23: The Face Behind the Mask

Emma's heart pounded as she stood in the doorway of the old library, the Spectator's hideout. Dust swirled in the faint light seeping through the cracked windows, casting eerie shadows across the bookshelves lined with decaying tomes. But her eyes weren't on the surroundings; they were fixed on the figure standing at the center of the room, facing away from her. The Spectator. Her breath caught in her throat as the figure slowly turned, the faint echo of his movements loud in the stillness of the room.

It was him. The man she had known for years, thought she could trust, someone she'd never suspected. Eric Stone. Her former mentor and the man who had taught her everything she knew about law enforcement. She struggled to process the sight of him now, clad in dark clothing, his eyes cold and calculating as he looked at her, devoid of any of the warmth she'd once known.

"You," she whispered, the disbelief coloring her voice. "Eric... it was you all along?"

Eric's face softened for a fleeting moment, the ghost of the man she'd respected and trusted flickering across his expression before the mask of indifference fell back into place. He nodded, letting out a slow sigh as if the weight of his secrets had finally settled over him, solid and undeniable. "I was wondering how long it would take for you to find me, Emma," he said, his voice steady. "But deep down, I think you already knew."

Emma shook her head, unable to reconcile the man in front of her with the respected officer who had been a guiding force throughout her career. "I don't understand," she managed, her voice cracking. "Why would you do this? All those people... you killed them, Eric. They had families, lives—"

"They were corrupt!" he shot back, the fire in his eyes startling her. "They were poison, eating away at this city. Every one of them abused their power, destroyed lives, and went unpunished. I just did what the system refused to do—held them accountable."

Emma felt a chill creep down her spine as she realized the depth of his conviction. "So you decided to become judge, jury, and executioner?" Her voice was barely a whisper, a mix of horror and betrayal. "That's not justice, Eric. That's murder."

His gaze hardened. "You don't know what it's like, Emma. I tried for years to change things from the inside, to fight the corruption the right way. But I kept hitting walls. Every step forward came with a hundred steps back. It broke me, and then... I lost her."

Emma's heart twisted at the mention. She knew who he was talking about: Sarah, his wife, a beloved member of the community who had been killed in a hit-and-run incident years before. The driver had been a well-known businessman with deep connections in the city's political sphere. Despite mounting evidence, he had never been charged, shielded by the very system Eric had sworn to serve. Emma had been there to support him through the pain, but she hadn't known the full extent of his grief—or the darkness it had sown within him.

"Sarah's death," he continued, voice thick with emotion, "was the breaking point. The man who killed her walked away free, while I was left picking up the pieces of a shattered life. And I realized, Emma... they were all like him. The people who destroy others' lives, protected by money, by power, by their connections. No one was going to bring them to justice. So I did it myself."

Emma's hands clenched at her sides. She couldn't deny the pain he had suffered or the injustice he had endured, but the weight of his crimes bore down on her. "You turned yourself into the very thing you hated, Eric. You became the corruption you despised."

A bitter smile tugged at the corners of his mouth. "I became what was necessary to end the cycle. You think this city's officials, the leaders you're so desperate to protect, are innocent? They're all part of it, Emma. Every single one."

Emma forced herself to stay focused, refusing to let his words twist her own convictions. "That doesn't give you the right to decide who lives and dies," she said, her voice steady. "You may have started with a cause, but this... this is a crusade driven by hate. You're no better than the people you went after."

For a moment, she thought she saw regret in his eyes, a flicker of the man she'd known, the mentor who had guided her through the challenges of her career. But it was gone as quickly as it had appeared, replaced by a hardened resolve.

"Emma," he said quietly, his voice almost gentle, "I'm not asking for your forgiveness. I never expected to be understood. But you have to see that this city will eat you alive if you keep playing by the rules. It's rotten to the core, and it always will be."

Emma's grip on her weapon tightened. "Maybe. But I'll take my chances. I won't let you hurt anyone else."

Eric's mouth twisted into a sad smile. "You were always one of the best, Emma. I knew you'd be the one to find me. But it's too late for us to turn back now. You know too much."

Her breath caught as he reached for something inside his jacket, but she was quicker. In a split second, she aimed her weapon, her finger hovering over the trigger. "Don't," she warned, her voice a razor-sharp edge.

But Eric merely held up his hands, as if in surrender, his gaze steady. "I had a feeling it would end like this," he murmured, his voice almost tender. "One way or another, I was prepared."

The silence between them stretched, thick with unspoken words, with the weight of a lifetime of loyalty, respect, and love twisted into something dark and tragic. Finally, Eric spoke again, his voice calm, almost resigned.

"If you pull that trigger, you'll be killing a man who once fought for justice, who lost everything to a broken system," he said, his gaze boring into her. "But if you let me go, if you allow me to finish this… I swear, it'll be the last thing I ever do."

Emma's resolve wavered as she looked into his eyes, searching for any sign of the man he had once been. She could feel the weight of her duty, the responsibility to bring him in, to see him face justice for the lives he had taken. But she also knew that, in his own twisted way, he had believed himself to be a savior, a guardian of the city. The lines between right and wrong, justice and vengeance, blurred until she could no longer tell where one ended and the other began.

"Eric," she said softly, almost pleading, "there's still a way back. You don't have to do this."

He shook his head slowly, a look of profound sadness in his eyes. "This is my path, Emma. And it's too late to turn around."

In that moment, she saw him for what he was: a man shattered by grief, driven to the edge of sanity by a quest for justice that had twisted into something monstrous. But behind the mask, behind the rage and the bloodshed, he was still Eric, the man who had once inspired her, who had once been her closest friend.

Her weapon lowered slightly, her hands trembling as she wrestled with the decision that would define her life. And as she stood there, frozen in place, Eric took a step back, his figure fading into the shadows, leaving her alone with the weight of the choice she had made.

Chapter 24: The Price of Truth

Emma stood alone in the dimly lit briefing room, her mind reeling from the revelations that had just unraveled before her. The files on the table were damning, exposing a web of corruption and deceit that stretched further than she could have ever imagined. Politicians, business tycoons, law enforcement officials—all implicated in the conspiracy that had given birth to the Spectator's twisted crusade. These people had hidden their crimes under layers of protection, and each line on the paper in front of her represented a life ruined, a family shattered, a crime covered up. She had all the pieces of the puzzle, finally, but now she had to decide what to do with them.

A knock on the door jolted her out of her thoughts, and she looked up to see Thorne, his face drawn and weary. He stepped inside, closing the door quietly behind him, and crossed his arms as he studied her, a mixture of worry and empathy in his eyes.

"Emma," he began cautiously, "I know what you're thinking. But you need to consider what this means. If you go public with this, the fallout... it'll be catastrophic. Not just for the people in these files, but for everyone who trusted them. The entire city could come undone."

Emma nodded, her fingers tracing the edges of the papers. She knew he was right. The cost of exposing the truth would be immense. Public confidence would crumble, and the collateral damage could be devastating, touching lives that had no part in the corruption. Yet, keeping it hidden would mean leaving the guilty unpunished, allowing the very rot that the Spectator had fought against to remain in place. She had to weigh the truth against the lives it could destroy.

Her silence spoke volumes, and Thorne stepped closer, lowering his voice. "Emma, is there another way? Is there a way we can take down the worst of them without pulling everyone else down too?"

"I don't know," she whispered, her voice breaking. "If I start covering for some of them, then where do I stop? If I play the game by their rules, I become one of them."

Thorne ran a hand through his hair, frustration evident in his movements. "Emma, I get it. But think about the innocent people, the ones who don't deserve to suffer because of this. We need a plan that limits the damage."

She felt a pang of guilt as she realized the implications of what he was saying. By choosing to reveal everything, she would be condemning the city to chaos, possibly even bloodshed. But if she hid the truth, then she was complicit in the corruption she despised. Her thoughts drifted to Eric, the man she'd once respected who had been willing to sacrifice everything, even his own soul, to bring justice to those who had escaped it.

Her fingers hovered over his name on one of the documents. She knew that he had tried to show her the cost of fighting for justice in a corrupt world. She could see the appeal of his approach now—taking down only those he deemed beyond redemption. Yet she couldn't bring herself to adopt his methods. She had to find another way, one that wouldn't compromise the very principles she stood for.

Thorne's voice broke through her thoughts again. "What if we selectively leak the information? Target just a few key people—make an example out of them. We expose the ones we can prove beyond a doubt are guilty, but keep the rest contained. It's not perfect, but it might be the best option we have."

Emma considered his suggestion, a glimmer of hope stirring within her. If they could limit the fallout, it might prevent the city from tearing itself apart. But even that plan felt like a betrayal of the full truth. She wanted justice, not selective vengeance. And yet, was she willing to sacrifice lives for the sake of absolute honesty?

As she struggled with her choice, she glanced at Thorne, seeing the weight of the decision reflected in his eyes. He had been with her every step of the way, had seen the darkness they were fighting against. He understood the gravity of what they were up against, and he was willing to stand by her, whatever choice she made.

Finally, she let out a slow breath. "I think... I think I'll have to do it Thorne's way," she said, her voice wavering. "We'll expose the ones we can confirm are guilty without any doubt. We make examples of the worst, let them take the fall for the others. It won't be the whole truth, but it will be enough to send a message."

Thorne gave her a reassuring nod, a hint of relief softening his expression. "We'll do it carefully, Emma. We'll make sure that justice is served without causing unnecessary harm. But you know this will be dangerous. They'll try to silence you once they realize what's happening."

Emma clenched her fists, a fierce determination hardening her resolve. "I'm ready for that. If they come after me, I'll be waiting. They can try to bury the truth, but I'll keep fighting, no matter the cost."

Together, they began sifting through the files, sorting out the evidence that would be the most damning, focusing on those who had committed the gravest crimes. Names like Councilman Hayes, CEO Howard Palmer, and Chief Deputy Robert Cross stood out, each of them guilty of abuses of power that had directly led to suffering and death. These would be the ones to fall, the ones who would bear the brunt of the public's outrage.

As they prepared the evidence for release, a quiet tension settled over them. They were playing a dangerous game, one that could cost them everything if it went wrong. But Emma felt a sense of purpose, a clarity that had eluded her throughout the investigation. She was finally taking control, fighting back against the forces that had sought to control her.

The following day, the first story broke. Headlines splashed across the news outlets, detailing the allegations against Councilman Hayes. Reporters dug into his background, unearthing connections to organized crime, money laundering, and more. Within hours, public outrage erupted. Protests gathered outside his office, demanding his resignation.

One by one, the other names began to fall. Palmer's corrupt business dealings were exposed, and Cross's involvement in covering up police brutality cases surfaced. The city was shocked, reeling from the depth of the betrayal. But with each revelation, Emma saw a glimmer of hope—a chance that maybe, just maybe, this could be the beginning of real change.

But as the days passed, she noticed something unsettling. Other officials, powerful figures whose names had been buried deep in her files, were quietly disappearing from the headlines. It was as if the system was protecting itself, shielding certain individuals from the fallout. Emma realized that her efforts, while impactful, had only scratched the surface. The deeper corruption was still untouched, lurking beneath the public's awareness, biding its time.

One evening, as she sat alone in her apartment, the weight of the truth settled over her once more. The battle was far from over, and she knew that more sacrifices would be required if she wanted to truly cleanse the city. But for now, she had dealt a powerful blow, had sent a message to those who thought themselves untouchable.

She would keep fighting, for the city and for the people who had been left voiceless for far too long. And she would continue to pay the price of truth, whatever it demanded of her.

Chapter 25: The Price of Redemption

Emma sat alone in her small, sparsely decorated apartment, staring at the empty glass in her hands. The quietness around her felt heavy, oppressive, pressing down on her in a way that was almost suffocating. The last few days had passed in a blur of headlines, accusations, and the fallout from the scandal that had shaken the entire city to its core. She'd done what she believed was right—she'd exposed the guilty, torn away the veil of secrecy that had shielded the corrupt for so long. But as she sat there in the silence, a gnawing doubt crept into her mind, one that she couldn't quite shake.

The headlines hadn't stopped since her revelations. Every day brought new details, new faces caught in the web of corruption she'd helped to expose. But now, as the dust began to settle, she found herself grappling with an emptiness she hadn't anticipated. Her mind drifted to the friends she'd lost along the way, relationships strained and broken by the choices she'd made. Her sense of duty had always driven her forward, but she couldn't deny the toll it had taken on her own life, on the people she'd pushed away, the trust she'd lost.

The knock at her door came unexpectedly, breaking the silence, and she felt a surge of apprehension as she rose to answer it. She opened the door to see Thorne standing there, his expression as weary as her own. He gave her a nod, a silent acknowledgment of the shared experiences they both bore. Without a word, she stepped aside to let him in.

Thorne surveyed the room, his gaze lingering on the few personal items she had: an old photograph of her parents, a stack of case files, the small plant she'd managed to keep alive against all odds. It felt odd to have him here, in her private space, and she realized how little of her life she had shared with anyone outside of her work.

"They're calling you a hero," he said finally, his voice breaking the silence. "The papers, the public—they think you're some kind of crusader."

Emma let out a hollow laugh. "Is that what they're calling it? I wonder if they'd still think that if they knew the cost."

Thorne nodded slowly, understanding evident in his eyes. "You did what you thought was right. You exposed the truth. That's more than most people would have had the courage to do."

"But at what price?" she asked, her voice barely more than a whisper. "I've lost everything, Thorne. My friends, my family... they look at me differently now. Even my own reflection feels like a stranger. I don't know if I can even recognize myself after all this."

He was silent for a moment, then he looked at her, his gaze steady. "Maybe redemption doesn't come easily, Emma. Maybe it means sacrificing a part of yourself for the greater good. But you've given people hope. You've shown them that the powerful aren't untouchable, that justice isn't just a hollow word."

Emma felt a pang of something—gratitude, perhaps—as she listened to his words. But it didn't erase the deep-seated unease within her. She wondered if justice truly had been served, or if all she'd done was temporarily disrupt a system too deeply rooted in its own corruption to ever truly change. Exposing the truth had been her mission, but now, standing in the wreckage of her own life, she couldn't help but wonder if it had all been worth it.

They stood in silence for a few minutes, the weight of their shared memories pressing down on them. Then, with a quiet sigh, Emma moved to the small table by her window and gestured for Thorne to join her. They sat together, each lost in their own thoughts, as the city lights twinkled in the distance, oblivious to the turmoil within her heart.

After a while, Thorne spoke again. "What will you do now?"

Emma glanced at him, a faint smile tugging at the corners of her mouth. "I don't know," she admitted. "Maybe it's time I stopped chasing after shadows, stopped trying to save a city that doesn't want to be saved. Or maybe... maybe I'll find a way to keep fighting, but on my own terms this time."

Thorne looked at her, something unspoken passing between them. "You've done enough, Emma. You don't have to carry this burden alone anymore."

For the first time, she felt the full weight of his words, the offer of solidarity, of companionship, that he was extending to her. It was a small comfort, but it was something. She'd spent so long trying to be the hero, trying to bear the weight of the city's sins, that she'd forgotten what it meant to have someone by her side.

As the night wore on, they talked quietly, sharing memories, laughter, even a few moments of silence that felt strangely comforting. Thorne's presence was a balm to her wounded spirit, a reminder that she wasn't entirely alone. They spoke of everything and nothing, of the future and the past, and as the hours slipped by, Emma felt a glimmer of hope—a faint, fragile hope that perhaps, in time, she could find a way to heal.

When Thorne finally left, she felt lighter somehow, as though a part of the weight she'd been carrying had lifted. She stood by the window, watching the first light of dawn creeping over the horizon, and felt a sense of peace that had eluded her for so long. The scars of the investigation would remain, she knew, but perhaps they didn't have to define her. Perhaps redemption wasn't something she had to chase after, but something she could find within herself, one step at a time.

She walked back to her desk and looked at the stack of files waiting for her, the remnants of the case that had nearly destroyed her. With a deep breath, she picked them up and placed them in a drawer, locking it shut. She wasn't sure what the future held, but she knew one thing: she was done letting the ghosts of the past haunt her.

For now, that was enough.

Chapter 26: The Deadly Game

Emma felt the tension in the air like a tangible weight pressing against her, an invisible clock ticking away each second as she moved through the dimly lit corridors of the abandoned building. Every instinct she had honed over the years screamed at her to leave, to retreat to the safety of her team, to regroup and come back with reinforcements. But she knew that the Spectator had orchestrated this final game with her as the centerpiece, and any delay could cost her everything. There was no going back.

Her phone buzzed in her pocket, and she pulled it out, her eyes narrowing as she read the message flashing across the screen: *Only one move left, Emma. Make it count.* She clenched her jaw, her gaze scanning her surroundings, assessing each shadow, each corner, aware that the Spectator could be watching, waiting for her to make a misstep.

The room she entered was empty, save for a chair in the center, a single light hanging above it, casting eerie shadows on the walls. As she approached, she saw a note taped to the back of the chair. She peeled it off and read the words written in a familiar, taunting scrawl: *The next clue is closer than you think.*

Emma's mind raced as she tried to decode the message. The Spectator's games had always been brutal, but this one was personal. He had spent months tracking her moves, dissecting her strengths and weaknesses, manipulating her at every turn. And now, he was drawing her into the heart of his final, deadly trap. She felt the weight of her choices as she considered her next steps, each decision carrying with it the potential to bring her closer to the Spectator or lead her into a carefully laid snare.

She took a deep breath and began examining the room. Her gaze drifted to the walls, the floor, searching for anything out of place. A faint gleam caught her eye—a small camera nestled in the corner, its red light blinking ominously. He was watching her. She forced herself to remain calm, to push aside the creeping unease, and focus on the task at hand. If he wanted her to make the next move, she would, but on her own terms.

Moving quietly, she turned her back to the camera and scanned the room with fresh eyes, her fingers brushing against the edges of the walls, searching for hidden compartments or false panels. The Spectator's games were always intricate, but there was a method to his madness, a pattern she could almost predict if she looked close enough. Her hand froze as she felt a slight shift in one of the wall panels. She pressed against it, and it clicked open, revealing a small compartment with another note inside.

You're so close, Emma. Just a few steps more, and all your questions will be answered.

Her pulse quickened as she pocketed the note and moved toward the door, her mind racing through the possibilities. She knew she was walking into a trap, but she was beyond caring. She needed to end this, to stop the Spectator once and for all. Every step she took felt like a countdown, her heart pounding as she ventured deeper into the maze of rooms, each one echoing with the silence that only heightened her awareness of how exposed she was.

Her phone buzzed again, another message illuminating the screen. *You're running out of time, Detective. Are you ready for the final reveal?*

The words sent a shiver down her spine, but she steadied herself, her mind focused, her senses sharp. She knew the Spectator was leading her somewhere specific, that every message, every clue was designed to push her to the edge, to test her resolve. The thought crossed her mind that he wanted her to be afraid, to feel vulnerable. But fear was a luxury she couldn't afford. She pushed forward, her eyes fixed on the narrow corridor stretching before her.

At the end of the hallway, she found a door slightly ajar, the faint glow of light spilling out from within. She hesitated for a fraction of a second, then stepped through, bracing herself for whatever lay beyond. The room was dark, save for a single spotlight illuminating a table in the center, where an assortment of objects lay scattered—photos, documents, a single gun resting at the edge. She recognized the faces in the photos, each one a victim of the Spectator, each one a piece of the puzzle she had spent months trying to solve.

She approached the table, her gaze shifting to the documents, her heart skipping a beat as she recognized her own name scrawled across several pages. Reports detailing her cases, her successes, her failures, even personal information that only someone who had been watching her closely could have known. The realization hit her with a sickening clarity: she wasn't just chasing the Spectator—she was his final target.

A voice crackled over a hidden speaker, low and mocking, filling the room with a sound that made her blood run cold. "Did you really think you could win this game, Emma? Did you really believe you could outsmart me?"

She clenched her fists, her voice steady as she replied, "I've come this far, haven't I? You've lost control, Spectator. You're just a coward hiding behind screens, behind walls. You can't hide forever."

The voice chuckled, a hollow, chilling sound that echoed around her. "Oh, but I've already won, Emma. Look at you—alone, vulnerable, clinging to the hope that you'll somehow escape this. But deep down, you know how this ends. You were always meant to be part of the story, just not in the way you imagined."

Her eyes scanned the room, searching for the source of the voice, her mind racing as she calculated her next move. She knew he was watching, that every gesture, every expression was being scrutinized, cataloged for his twisted sense of amusement. But she wouldn't give him the satisfaction of seeing her break.

"You think you've won because you've managed to stay in the shadows," she replied, her voice laced with defiance. "But shadows don't last. Sooner or later, the light finds them. And when it does, I'll be there."

The silence stretched for a moment, then the voice spoke again, its tone sharper, more controlled. "You're running out of time, Emma. The final choice is yours—walk away and live with the guilt, or take the gun and finish this once and for all. Either way, you'll never be free of me."

Her gaze drifted to the gun on the table, a cold, metallic reminder of the choices she'd made to reach this point. She felt the weight of the Spectator's challenge, the temptation to end this once and for all, to silence the voice that had haunted her for so long. But something in her refused to give in, a stubborn resilience that had carried her through every hardship, every loss.

She took a step back, her voice steady as she made her final stand. "You don't control me, Spectator. I don't need your games, your twisted sense of justice. This ends now, not because you say so, but because I choose to walk away."

The lights flickered, the room plunging into darkness, the voice fading into an eerie silence. For a moment, she felt the weight of his gaze, the invisible presence of a predator realizing its prey had escaped. And then, with a final click, the room was empty, the Spectator's game over, his voice silenced at last.

Chapter 27: The Haunting Truth

Emma sat at her desk, the dim light of dawn filtering through the blinds and casting long shadows across the room. Her eyes were fixed on the case files sprawled before her, documents scattered haphazardly, as if by putting them together in the right order, she could finally make sense of everything. But each piece only served to deepen the unsettling feeling in her gut, the gnawing suspicion that she hadn't seen the Spectator's true intentions until now.

For months, she had followed his trail, tracing each murder, each meticulously planned message, believing it was a mission to expose corruption, to force the city to reckon with its darkest secrets. But what lay before her now was an ugly truth—one she hadn't been prepared to confront. The evidence didn't point to justice; it pointed to revenge.

She picked up a photograph, one of the few still intact after a long night of combing through evidence. The picture showed a woman with a gentle smile, standing beside a young man—her son, as Emma had come to learn. The Spectator's first victim, a man she'd once believed was a corrupt official, was this woman's husband. And it was that connection—seemingly so insignificant at the time—that had led her here. The Spectator's crusade wasn't about making the world better; it was about making those who wronged him suffer.

She leaned back, letting out a heavy breath as the revelation settled over her. All of it—the methodical brutality, the elaborate puzzles, the hints at some greater purpose—was nothing more than a façade. The Spectator wasn't acting out of any sense of morality or desire to expose corruption. This was vengeance, pure and simple. He had constructed a web of lies so intricate that even she, with all her training and instincts, had failed to see through it until now.

Her mind reeled as she went over the other victims, each of whom had seemed carefully chosen. Businessmen, politicians, law enforcement—she'd thought they shared a connection of corruption. But now she saw the real link: each of them had, in some way, been responsible for a tragedy that had struck the Spectator's own life, a sequence of events that had turned him from an ordinary man into a meticulous killer with a vendetta.

One by one, she revisited each case, the pieces falling into place in a horrifying clarity. The first victim, a prominent businessman, had been linked to an investment scheme that collapsed, costing hundreds of families their savings—including the Spectator's. The second, a high-ranking police official, had overseen an investigation that dismissed allegations of corruption tied to that same company, leaving those affected with no recourse. Each of the Spectator's targets had played a role in the systemic failures that had destroyed lives.

Emma clenched her fists as anger built up inside her. She'd been chasing an illusion, believing that her relentless pursuit was uncovering something meaningful, something that would bring about change. But the Spectator had twisted her sense of purpose, using her to enact his own dark, private retribution under the guise of justice. Every victim, every step of the way, had been part of a meticulously planned execution of his personal vendetta.

Her thoughts turned to her own team, to the way the investigation had taken a toll on all of them. She recalled the sleepless nights, the fear and frustration, the moments where she questioned her own judgment. And now, here she was, realizing that it had all been a pawn in the Spectator's game, each move pushing her closer to this devastating conclusion.

A knock on the door pulled her out of her thoughts. Detective Thorne stepped in, his expression grim as he looked at her. He didn't need to say anything; the look in his eyes told her he'd reached the same conclusion.

"It was never about the city, was it?" he said, his voice barely above a whisper.

Emma shook her head. "No. It was always about him. We just didn't see it."

Thorne took a seat across from her, rubbing his temples as he processed the revelation. "We thought we were chasing someone trying to expose the truth. But he was just hiding his own darkness behind that image, using us to get what he wanted."

Emma's gaze drifted to the stack of evidence before her. "And we were so close to buying into it. It was all so carefully constructed—every step designed to make us believe we were unraveling something bigger. But it was only a lie, a cover for his own revenge."

She could see the weariness etched into Thorne's face, the same exhaustion she felt pressing down on her shoulders. They had invested so much, convinced that they were making a difference, only to find that they'd been manipulated from the start.

"What now?" he asked quietly.

Emma leaned forward, her jaw set with determination. "We finish this. We bring him in. No matter what he's done, he can't hide behind his own twisted sense of justice. People deserve to know the truth."

Thorne nodded, but Emma could see the doubt in his eyes, the weight of the journey they'd been through together. "The city won't look at us the same way after this. We were his pawns, part of his plan. He wanted us to find him, to expose what he'd done under his terms."

"Maybe," Emma replied, her voice resolute. "But that doesn't mean we don't do our jobs. We can't control what the city thinks. But we can make sure he doesn't get away with this."

They sat in silence, each lost in their own thoughts, as the weight of their discovery settled over them. The realization that the man they'd been hunting had played them so perfectly was a bitter pill to swallow, a haunting truth that would linger long after the case was closed.

Finally, Emma rose from her seat, gathering the files and stacking them neatly, each document a reminder of the price they'd paid for answers. She had thought that the Spectator's motives would reveal something about the city's corruption, a higher purpose that would justify the sacrifices they'd made. But instead, they'd uncovered something far darker: a man driven by vengeance, willing to destroy anything and anyone who stood in his way, even if it meant manipulating those who had trusted him.

"Let's go," she said, her voice steady, though her heart felt heavy. "We still have a job to do."

As they left the room, Emma couldn't shake the sense that something fundamental had shifted within her. The Spectator had shown her that justice wasn't always pure, that sometimes, even those who claimed to act for the greater good could be corrupted by their own pain. And as much as she wanted to believe that they could still make a difference, she knew that the haunting truth of this case would stay with her, a shadow cast over every choice she made from this moment on.

Chapter 28: The Final Confrontation

Emma approached the abandoned warehouse, her pulse steady despite the adrenaline coursing through her veins. The structure loomed dark and silent, tucked away in a forgotten corner of the city where no one would hear or intervene in what was about to unfold. She was alone, by her own choice—knowing that no one else should face the Spectator. It was her case, her responsibility, and now, the inevitable final confrontation.

She took a deep breath, gripping her weapon tightly as she slipped through a side entrance. The dim light filtering through broken windows cast eerie shadows, playing tricks on her eyes. The silence was oppressive, broken only by the faint drip of water somewhere in the distance. Emma moved cautiously, her senses alert, knowing the Spectator could be watching her every step. She had studied his movements, his messages, and his targets, but here, in the heart of his chosen lair, it was his game. She knew he had lured her here for a reason, to face her one last time on his terms.

As she crept forward, she became acutely aware of the significance of this moment. Every victim, every clue, every sleepless night had led her here. She rounded a corner, and then, as if on cue, the lights flared to life, flooding the vast open space. Emma squinted, her eyes adjusting to the sudden brightness, and then she saw him. Standing in the center of the warehouse, a calm and almost serene expression on his face, was the Spectator.

"Detective Carter," he greeted her, his voice echoing off the walls. His tone was casual, almost friendly, as though they were old acquaintances meeting under far different circumstances.

Emma held her stance, her weapon trained on him. "This ends now. I'm not here to talk."

He smiled, a slow, mocking smile that sent a chill down her spine. "Oh, I think you are, Emma. After everything, you must be curious. You've followed my trail, uncovered my secrets. You know the truth now—why I did what I did."

She studied him, her mind racing as she calculated her next move. "You killed innocent people. Destroyed lives. All for some twisted sense of revenge. Justice? You have no idea what that word even means."

The Spectator's expression hardened, his eyes flashing with something darker. "Justice?" he scoffed. "I spent my life believing in that illusion. But justice is a myth, a convenient story we tell ourselves to sleep at night. I didn't do this to serve justice—I did this to reveal the truth."

Emma shook her head, keeping her gaze fixed on him. "Your 'truth' is just your own pain, your own vendetta. You destroyed people who had families, who didn't deserve to die. You're not a crusader, you're a murderer."

He tilted his head, considering her words. "Is that what you believe? After all you've seen, after everything you've uncovered? Tell me, Emma—can you honestly say that these people didn't deserve punishment? That they were innocent?"

Emma's jaw clenched, and she forced herself to remain steady. She couldn't let him get inside her head. She had to stay focused. But his words gnawed at her, pressing into the corners of her mind. She thought of the corruption, the cover-ups, the lives ruined by people who wielded power with impunity. The city was a broken place, and he had exploited that weakness, weaponizing it for his own purposes.

"They weren't saints," she said finally. "But that doesn't justify what you did. You took the law into your own hands, made yourself judge, jury, and executioner. You're no better than the people you targeted."

He chuckled, a low, mirthless sound. "I'm no better? Maybe not. But at least I didn't pretend to be. I looked at this city and saw it for what it truly is—a place where people like us don't matter, where justice is reserved for those who can afford it. You of all people should understand that, Emma."

She felt her resolve waver for just a moment, but then she pushed back. "I didn't join this job to play God. You twisted everything, manipulated innocent people to fuel your own hatred. That's not the truth—that's a sickness."

The Spectator took a step forward, his gaze intense, piercing. "And yet, here you are, Emma, still pursuing me. You've followed my every move, obsessed over my motives. Maybe it's because deep down, you understand why I did it. You see the same cracks in the system, the same rot. You know what I did was necessary."

Emma's grip tightened on her weapon, but his words struck a nerve. She couldn't deny that she had wrestled with doubts throughout this case, questions about the system she'd sworn to protect. But what he was suggesting—that she was somehow complicit, that his actions were justified—was something she couldn't accept.

She took a step closer, her voice steady. "No. I did my job. I fought to find you because you're a danger to this city. And I'll keep fighting to stop people like you from tearing it apart."

The Spectator's smile faded, replaced by a look of disappointment. "Then you're a fool, Emma. This city doesn't want saving. It thrives on corruption, on the very things you claim to stand against. You're just a cog in the machine, nothing more."

He reached into his coat, and for a brief second, Emma's heart pounded as she anticipated a weapon. But he pulled out a small notebook, tossing it onto the ground between them. "Everything I did, every decision, every target—it's all there. Read it, if you dare. See the truth for yourself."

Emma didn't take her eyes off him, but she glanced at the notebook, lying innocuously on the cold concrete. It was a trap, she knew that much, but a part of her was drawn to it, curious. The temptation to understand, to uncover the final pieces of his twisted logic, was almost overwhelming.

He took another step back, watching her with a strange mixture of pity and disdain. "You'll never win, Detective Carter. You can kill me, arrest me, but you can't change the city. It's bigger than both of us. It's untouchable."

Emma took a deep breath, steadying herself, and in that moment, she realized what she had to do. She didn't need his notebook, his explanations, or his twisted rationale. She had come here to put an end to his reign of terror, to stop him from hurting anyone else. No more games, no more words.

She raised her weapon, her voice cold and resolute. "This is over."

The Spectator raised his hands, a mocking smile on his face as if daring her to pull the trigger. "Go ahead, Emma. Prove me right. Show the world that even the 'good guys' aren't above a little bloodshed when it suits them."

But Emma didn't waver. She lowered her weapon slightly, stepping forward with purpose. "You're coming in, alive. You don't get to choose the terms anymore."

His expression faltered, just for a moment, as he realized she wouldn't give him the satisfaction of ending his life on his terms. The last of his power slipped away, and in that instant, he looked almost human, vulnerable. She took a pair of handcuffs from her belt, securing him as he glared at her, his eyes filled with a mix of anger and frustration.

As she led him out of the warehouse, the echoes of their encounter reverberated in her mind. She knew that his words would linger, that his dark ideology would haunt her long after this case was over. But she also knew that she'd made the right choice, that she had refused to be drawn into his twisted narrative.

For now, at least, justice had been served—not his version, but the kind she believed in, the kind that didn't bend to the darkness. And as she stepped out into the cold morning light, she felt a sense of clarity, a reminder of why she'd chosen this path, no matter how treacherous it had become.

Chapter 29: Aftermath and Reflection

The precinct was quieter than usual, a silence that clung to the walls, resonating with an unspoken grief. Emma sat at her desk, her hands resting idly on the cold surface as she stared at the empty whiteboard that once displayed every grisly detail of the Spectator's reign of terror. The photos had been taken down, the map cleared of pins. The investigation was over, yet the echoes of it remained, lingering in every corner of the office like a shadow.

She picked up a report on her desk, half-reading the words that summarized the events in clinical detail. Facts and figures that felt hollow compared to the reality she had lived. Each sentence seemed detached from the memories that now haunted her—a grim record that, for anyone else, would tell of a successful case, but for her, it told of a personal toll that went far beyond her badge.

Around her, her team moved with a palpable weariness. They were trying to return to their routines, to settle back into the everyday rhythm of police work. But the Spectator case had left them all changed, worn down by weeks of relentless pursuit and grim revelations. Ramirez's normally cheerful demeanor had dulled, his jokes falling flat. Collins, usually the calmest in the group, had been avoiding eye contact, lost in his own thoughts. And Moore—the rookie who had joined them barely a year ago—now wore a hardened expression that no training manual could prepare anyone for.

Emma's phone vibrated on her desk, pulling her out of her thoughts. A news alert. She glanced at it, the headline confirming what she already knew: "Spectator Case Ends; Public Trust in Law Enforcement Shaken." She put the phone down, her chest tightening at the reminder. The Spectator's actions had struck a deep blow, not only against the victims he targeted but against the very fabric of the city's trust in its protectors. People were asking questions, doubting if the institutions they had relied upon for security were truly there to protect them. Citizens wanted answers, and Emma wasn't sure she had any left to give.

She had devoted herself entirely to finding him, to stopping the cycle of violence he had set in motion. But now, in the stillness that followed the case's explosive end, doubts began to creep in. She wondered if she had done enough or, perhaps, gone too far. There were moments in the investigation when her anger had clouded her judgment, moments when the need to stop him had overridden everything else, including her own moral boundaries. Her pursuit of justice had been relentless, but at what cost?

"Emma?" a voice interrupted her thoughts. It was Ramirez, standing by her desk with a tentative expression. He looked at her with a mixture of empathy and exhaustion, as if he too had been wrestling with the weight of the case. "We're heading out to grab some coffee. Want to join?"

She hesitated, her instinct telling her to decline, to retreat back into the solitude she'd carved out for herself these past few days. But then she nodded, standing up and grabbing her coat. Maybe a moment away from the precinct would help, even if just for a little while.

They walked in silence to a nearby café, the quiet streets reflecting the city's unease. People glanced at them with expressions of suspicion and doubt, subtle but undeniable. It was as if the case had left an invisible scar on the city, one that even strangers on the street could sense.

Inside the café, they ordered their drinks and found a table in the corner. Emma stared into her coffee, the steam rising like a ghostly reminder of all the unresolved feelings she carried. Ramirez leaned forward, breaking the silence.

"It's strange, isn't it?" he said, his voice low. "We spent so long chasing him, but now that it's over, it doesn't feel... finished."

Emma looked up, meeting his gaze. "That's because it isn't finished, not really. We stopped the Spectator, but the damage he caused, the questions he raised... they're still out there. People are scared. They're doubting us, and maybe they should be."

Ramirez frowned, his expression a mixture of frustration and sorrow. "You did everything you could, Emma. We all did. But I get it. I feel it too—the weight of it. This case... it's like it's going to haunt us forever."

She nodded, grateful for his honesty. "I know. But it's more than that. For the first time, I'm not sure if what we did was enough, or if we crossed a line trying to stop him. He made us question everything—our purpose, our methods. I used to believe that justice was clear, black and white. Now, I'm not so sure."

Ramirez took a deep breath, letting her words sink in. "He wanted us to doubt ourselves, to doubt the system. That was part of his game. But we're not like him, Emma. We made mistakes, sure, but we're still here, still trying to do what's right. That has to mean something."

Emma's gaze drifted to the window, where people walked by, unaware of the turmoil that had gripped the city just days ago. The Spectator had exposed the city's fragility, the fine line between order and chaos. And in doing so, he had forced her to confront her own limits, her own weaknesses.

"He believed that justice was an illusion," she said, almost to herself. "That we're all just pretending, hiding behind our badges and our laws. And maybe he was right, at least about some things. There are flaws in the system, corruption, people who exploit their power. But that doesn't mean we give up."

Ramirez nodded, his expression resolute. "If we give up, he wins. That's what he wanted all along—to make us question ourselves until we lose faith in what we're doing. But that's not who we are."

Emma felt a glimmer of resolve settle in her chest, a reminder of why she had chosen this path, even knowing its challenges. The Spectator had tried to break her, to make her doubt herself and the purpose she served. But as she sat there, surrounded by the quiet resilience of her team, she realized that she wasn't alone. They had all faced this trial together, and they would continue to stand together, even in the aftermath.

When they returned to the precinct, Emma felt a new determination. There was still work to be done—rebuilding trust, answering the city's questions, and ensuring that justice was served not just in theory but in practice. She knew it wouldn't be easy, that the scars of this case would linger for a long time. But she also knew that she had the strength to face it, to learn from the darkness they had all been through.

As she took her seat at her desk once more, Emma glanced at the empty whiteboard. The Spectator's case was closed, but the impact of his actions would be felt for years to come. And yet, in that moment, she felt a quiet sense of purpose reignite within her—a commitment to continue, to fight for justice, no matter how blurred the lines might become.

Chapter 30: The Weight of Betrayal

Emma sat alone in the interrogation room, a heavy silence pressing down on her. The stark, sterile walls around her seemed to close in, amplifying the bitterness she felt. Betrayal. She had always known it was possible, always understood that the line between friend and foe could blur, especially in their line of work. But knowing it in theory and experiencing it firsthand were entirely different things. The discovery of corruption within her own department was a bitter pill to swallow, and one she could still hardly believe. People she had trusted, people she had worked beside for years, had been working against her, obstructing her pursuit of justice.

As the weight of that realization settled, Emma clenched her fists, anger and disbelief warring within her. The Spectator's twisted influence had reached deeper than she had ever imagined. Every revelation about his network, every confession, had led to yet another hidden layer of corruption, implicating people she would have sworn were loyal, people she'd never have thought capable of deceit. It was almost as if he had known the system better than she did, as if he had been a part of it all along, maneuvering unseen in the dark corridors of her own precinct.

The door to the interrogation room opened, and Collins stepped in. His face was solemn, but Emma could see the traces of guilt there as well. Collins had been one of the few officers who had stuck by her, loyal to the case, determined to uncover the truth, no matter how painful. And yet, even his unwavering presence felt tainted now, a reminder of just how close the corruption had come to her inner circle.

"We just finished going over the files," he said, his voice quiet. "It's worse than we thought, Emma. Some of the officers... they've been taking bribes for years, covering up evidence, manipulating cases. And the Spectator—he knew it all. He was using it."

Emma looked at him, her eyes hard. "And we were blind to it. All of us. We let him play us, manipulate us, while he built his network right under our noses. How could we have missed it?"

Collins shook his head, the frustration evident on his face. "It's not your fault. He was careful, methodical. He knew where to strike, who to target. This wasn't just an attack on the victims; it was an attack on all of us. On everything we stand for."

Emma exhaled sharply, the anger inside her simmering just below the surface. "That's the problem, Collins. He knew exactly where to strike because he knew who would cover for him. People we trusted. People we relied on."

A brief silence stretched between them, both of them weighed down by the gravity of the situation. Emma could see the hurt in Collins's eyes too, a shared sense of betrayal that made her feel just a little less alone in her disillusionment. But she also knew that, despite his loyalty, trust was no longer something she could give so freely. It was a luxury she could no longer afford.

"Have you spoken to Ramirez?" Collins asked, breaking the silence.

Emma shook her head, avoiding his gaze. "Not yet. After the Spectator's final game, I'm not sure what's left to say. I thought I could trust him. I thought he was... different."

Collins placed a hand on her shoulder, his voice soft but resolute. "Emma, Ramirez was as blindsided as the rest of us. He's one of the good ones, you know that."

She let out a bitter laugh, shrugging his hand away. "Is he? Are any of us? I can't help but wonder if we're all just pawns in some twisted game. Maybe we're all guilty in some way, whether we realize it or not."

Collins's expression hardened, and for a moment, he looked as if he wanted to argue. But then he nodded, a resigned acceptance in his eyes. "I don't blame you for feeling that way. After everything we've been through, it's hard to know who to trust."

Emma met his gaze, a flicker of determination sparking within her. "But I'm not giving up, Collins. Not on this. Not on justice. The Spectator might have exposed the rot in our system, but that doesn't mean we let it fester. We clean it up, every last bit of it."

Collins nodded, a small smile tugging at the corners of his mouth. "I wouldn't expect anything less from you, Emma."

As he left the room, Emma was left alone once more, her thoughts racing. She felt the weight of the betrayal like a physical ache, a gnawing doubt that threatened to erode the foundation of everything she believed in. But she also felt a renewed sense of purpose, a drive to rebuild what the Spectator had tried to tear down.

Later that day, she called a meeting with her team. She knew they were just as shaken as she was, and perhaps even more so after discovering the depth of the corruption within their ranks. As they gathered around the conference table, their faces somber, she addressed them with a steely resolve.

"We've all been through hell these past few months," she began, her voice steady. "We've faced betrayal from those we trusted, seen the worst parts of our own department exposed. And I know that some of you are questioning everything right now. I am too."

She paused, looking around at each of them. "But we can't let this destroy us. We're here because we believe in justice, in protecting those who can't protect themselves. And that hasn't changed. Yes, there are people who failed us, people who betrayed us. But we have a choice now. We can either let this break us, or we can use it to make us stronger."

Moore, the rookie who had been so eager to prove himself, looked up, a determined glint in his eyes. "I'm with you, Emma. Whatever it takes, we'll rebuild this team, rebuild the trust we lost."

One by one, the others echoed his sentiment, a spark of hope igniting in the room. Emma felt a flicker of pride, her own doubts easing just a bit as she saw the resolve in their faces. They had been through the fire, but they were still standing.

After the meeting, Emma returned to her desk, feeling the weight of betrayal lessen, if only slightly. The Spectator had tried to tear them apart, to make them question everything they stood for. But he had underestimated their resilience, their determination to fight back. She knew it would be a long road ahead, that trust would not be rebuilt overnight. But she also knew that they would endure, that they would rise above the shadows he had cast over them.

As she sat in the quiet of the precinct, a sense of calm washed over her. She understood now that trust was something that had to be earned, something she would no longer give lightly. But she also understood that, despite everything, there was a strength in her team that could not be broken. And with that strength, she was ready to face whatever came next.

Chapter 31: The Final Revelation

Emma leaned back in her chair, allowing herself a rare moment of satisfaction. The case was closed, the Spectator apprehended, and the city could finally breathe a sigh of relief. The events of the past months had taken a toll on her, but in this moment, Emma felt a weight lift from her shoulders. Justice had been served, and the darkness that had shadowed the department was finally clearing. Yet, as she collected her belongings, preparing to leave the precinct for the first full night of rest in what felt like years, her phone buzzed.

It was Moore. "Detective Hale," he began, a nervous edge in his voice, "there's something you need to see. Evidence room. It's... strange."

With a weary sigh, Emma turned back, heading to the evidence room with a sense of foreboding she couldn't shake. Moore was waiting just outside, his face pale as he handed her a sealed plastic bag. Inside was a leather-bound notebook, worn around the edges but still familiar. She recognized it immediately. It was Inspector Thorne's.

Emma felt a jolt of confusion and disbelief. Thorne, her mentor, had been a solid presence throughout the entire investigation, his advice steady and unwavering. She remembered him pulling her aside, encouraging her to follow her instincts even when the case grew convoluted and disheartening. And now, standing here, she held a piece of evidence connected to him.

"I thought this was in his office," she said aloud, though mostly to herself. She looked at Moore, but he simply shrugged, just as bewildered.

"We found it with some of the Spectator's belongings," Moore said. "It was tucked inside one of the boxes from the final crime scene. We almost missed it, but..." He trailed off, casting Emma a concerned glance. "Do you think... could Thorne have known more about the Spectator's plans than he let on?"

Emma's mind raced. Thorne had been the first to alert her to the Spectator's pattern, to hint that this case was more than just a series of isolated crimes. He'd always seemed two steps ahead, guiding her as only a seasoned detective could. But could that guidance have concealed a deeper involvement? She dismissed the thought almost immediately. This was Thorne, the man who had been like a father to her, who had taught her everything she knew about justice.

She flipped open the notebook, her hands trembling slightly as she skimmed the pages. They were filled with notes, meticulous observations of the case, thoughts on suspects, sketches of the crime scenes—the kinds of things Thorne would jot down in his personal shorthand. But as she reached the last few pages, her breath caught. There, written in Thorne's unmistakable handwriting, were the words: *The game has only begun. The Spectator will not be the last.*

Emma's heart pounded as she read the chilling phrase over and over. Why would Thorne have written something like that? Was it a warning he hadn't yet had the chance to share, or had he kept it hidden intentionally? Questions surged through her mind, doubts she never imagined she'd entertain. Had Thorne known about the Spectator's motives all along? Or worse—had he been complicit in them?

Trying to steady herself, she turned to Moore. "Don't mention this to anyone yet. I need to handle it carefully."

Moore nodded, the unease in his eyes mirroring her own. Emma left the evidence room, clutching the notebook as though it held the answer to everything. She returned to her office and began poring over the pages, hoping to find some logical explanation. Yet, the more she read, the more unsettling the implications became. She began to recall subtle moments, small gestures she had overlooked, words of caution that had seemed protective at the time but now felt tainted with hidden intent.

The next day, she paid an unannounced visit to Thorne's apartment, a gnawing sense of betrayal urging her forward. She told herself it was simply due diligence, a way to cross off a possibility that no longer seemed so impossible. She told herself she wasn't here to dig into her mentor's life, but rather to prove his innocence once and for all.

She let herself in with the spare key Thorne had given her years ago, a gesture of trust that now felt hauntingly ironic. As she moved through his apartment, she found herself scrutinizing every detail, every book and photograph, wondering what secrets they might hide. On his desk, she found stacks of paperwork from the Spectator case, photos and profiles of the victims pinned to a board on the wall.

It all seemed typical, the work of a dedicated detective. But then she noticed a map, one she hadn't seen before. Pinned on it were locations she recognized from the case, but also several others that hadn't been connected to the Spectator's victims. These were unmarked, seemingly random places in the city. Why would Thorne be interested in these?

She took photos of the map and quickly left, her mind spinning with questions. Back at the station, she pulled up reports on the additional locations she'd seen marked on Thorne's map. Her stomach twisted as she realized what they were: abandoned sites, each tied to the Spectator's string of attacks. A few had been reported as having evidence tampering, as though someone had been erasing traces left behind. If Thorne had known about these sites, why hadn't he mentioned them? Why hadn't he followed up?

The final pieces began to fall into place, painting a picture she desperately wished wasn't true. It seemed impossible, yet the evidence was mounting. Could Thorne have been manipulating the investigation, subtly steering her to only see parts of the truth, keeping certain details hidden to prolong the game?

She thought back to his warnings, his insistence on the Spectator being a "necessary evil" in a city riddled with corruption. At the time, she had brushed it off as the pessimism of a veteran detective, but now it sounded almost like justification, as though he had rationalized the Spectator's methods. A part of her still clung to the hope that there was an explanation, that Thorne would have some rational answer for everything. But the weight of doubt pressed down on her, heavy and unyielding.

As evening fell, she sat in her office, staring at the collection of files in front of her. She had gathered everything—Thorne's notes, the map, the notebook, the evidence linking him indirectly to the Spectator. She knew what she had to do, but the thought of confronting Thorne, of accusing him of such a betrayal, felt like an insurmountable task. How could she face the man who had been her guide, her mentor, and now potentially, her enemy?

Taking a deep breath, she picked up her phone and dialed his number. After a few rings, Thorne's familiar voice answered, warm and steady as always.

"Emma," he greeted. "What's the matter? I didn't expect to hear from you tonight."

Her voice felt thick in her throat, but she forced herself to speak. "I found something, Inspector. Something that makes me wonder how much you really knew about the Spectator."

There was a pause on the line, a silence that stretched painfully before he responded, his tone calm but cautious. "Emma, that's a serious accusation. Why don't we meet, talk this over face-to-face?"

A chill ran down her spine at his tone, and she realized with a start that she no longer trusted him. "Where?" she asked, her voice low.

Thorne named a location, an old diner where they used to meet for coffee on their days off. She agreed, her mind racing with anticipation and dread. As she ended the call, she knew she was on the verge of uncovering the final piece of the puzzle, the one that would confirm or shatter everything she thought she knew about her mentor. And as she prepared to confront him, she steeled herself for whatever truth awaited her on the other side.

Chapter 32: The Shadow in the Ranks

Emma sat alone in her apartment, the dim glow from her computer casting a stark light across her face. She scrolled through files, notes, anything that might explain the connection between Thorne and the Spectator's victims. She began to see a pattern, faint but undeniable. Thorne had quietly overseen investigations in several cases where powerful figures had skirted justice—figures who, coincidentally, had been targeted by the Spectator. Each case file painted a picture of individuals tied to criminal activities, somehow evading consequence until the Spectator brought them down.

Emma's gaze sharpened as she opened a document that detailed Thorne's career, which seemed to cross paths with certain powerful names that had thrived in the shadows. It struck her that each figure in these cases—corrupt officials, untouchable criminals—had benefited from an unusual lack of scrutiny within the force. What if the Spectator had been doing what the justice system wouldn't, or couldn't? And what if Thorne had known all along?

She had to tread carefully. Her movements, her questions, even the files she accessed, would all be noticed by the wrong people if she wasn't cautious. She reached for her phone, dialing a trusted former colleague who had left the force years ago after rumors of corruption surfaced. Lou Reilly picked up on the second ring.

"Emma?" he asked, surprise evident in his voice.

"I need information, Lou. Off the record," she said quietly, scanning her empty apartment as if the walls had ears.

"Go on," he replied, instantly cautious but curious.

"Did you ever hear about a network within the force, a group that looked the other way on certain cases?" She could almost hear Lou stiffen on the other end.

"Emma," he sighed, "that's dangerous ground."

"Lou, I found something. I think Thorne is involved, and I think this network is real." Silence stretched for a beat.

"You're right to be careful," he finally said, his voice dropping to a near whisper. "The group you're talking about, some of us called them the 'Shadow

Network.' They've been around a long time, Emma, and they don't like people getting too close."

"Who's in it?" she pressed.

"High-ranking officials, some with badges, some without. Lawyers, judges, anyone who has something to gain by keeping certain crimes hidden. Thorne..." He hesitated. "Thorne used to be seen with some of these guys, but I thought he was different. Maybe he kept his head down, but it's possible he got roped in deeper than any of us realized."

Emma thanked Lou, her pulse racing. Her mind spun with the implications. Thorne had been her mentor, her guiding light in a murky system, but if he was part of this shadow organization, then he wasn't just an accomplice—he was complicit in keeping corruption alive in their city.

The next day, she went to the precinct but steered clear of her usual office. Instead, she headed down to the archives, where records from decades past were stored. She combed through cases, looking for discrepancies in investigations that Thorne had been part of. Patterns started to emerge. Cases that should have ended in convictions had stalled or mysteriously fizzled out, while other cases—particularly those that involved vulnerable victims—had been swept under the rug.

As she flipped through yet another file, a familiar voice sounded from the doorway. "Emma, what are you doing here?"

Emma looked up, startled to find Inspector Thorne standing there, watching her with a bemused expression. Her heart pounded as she tried to hide the wave of guilt that flashed across her face. "Research," she managed, her voice steadier than she felt.

"Research?" Thorne raised an eyebrow, his eyes narrowing as he took in the scattered files on the desk. "On old cases?"

Emma swallowed, forcing a casual tone. "Just some loose ends. Things I was curious about."

He stepped closer, his gaze lingering on the files, his expression unreadable. "Loose ends can be dangerous, Emma. You know that better than most."

She nodded, doing her best to appear unaffected, but her mind was racing. Thorne's words carried an unspoken warning, and she felt a pang of betrayal twist in her chest. Did he suspect her suspicions? Did he know how close she was to uncovering his involvement?

That night, she continued her investigation in secret, piecing together a timeline of Thorne's career and the individuals who had benefited from the Spectator's brand of vigilante justice. She began to see just how interconnected this network was, and how the Spectator's actions had shaken it. But with each revelation, the lines between good and evil blurred. How many lives had this "Shadow Network" ruined? And had the Spectator, in targeting them, merely attempted to correct a system that was deeply broken?

Emma was exhausted but resolute as dawn approached. She now understood the depth of the corruption within her own ranks, a shadowy infrastructure that had propped up some of the city's most notorious criminals and protected others for decades. And Thorne had been part of it all.

Determined to confront him, Emma arranged to meet Thorne in an isolated part of the city, away from prying eyes. She needed answers, and she was tired of dancing around the truth. Thorne arrived as requested, his expression guarded but calm as he stepped out of his car. He looked at Emma with an expression that seemed a mixture of wariness and regret.

"You've been digging, haven't you?" he asked.

"Yes," she replied evenly. "And I found a lot more than I ever wanted to know. I know about the Shadow Network, Thorne. I know you were part of it."

He sighed, rubbing a hand over his face. "Emma, you're still so young. You don't understand what it's like, trying to keep order in a city like this."

"Order?" she shot back, anger flaring in her chest. "You let criminals walk free, and you turned a blind eye when they hurt people. You can't justify that."

Thorne held her gaze, his face hardening. "I did what I had to, Emma. This city chews people up and spits them out. Sometimes, the only way to survive is to make compromises."

"Compromises?" She took a step closer, the weight of her betrayal driving her forward. "You protected them. You were supposed to protect us, protect justice, not them."

He shook his head, his voice taking on a steely edge. "The system is broken, Emma. I tried to fix it from within. The Spectator, whoever they were, only sped things along. I thought maybe, just maybe, they'd do what we couldn't."

Emma's mind raced as she processed his words. "So you knew. You knew who the Spectator was all along?"

Thorne's eyes flickered, betraying a sliver of guilt. "I had my suspicions. Maybe even had contact with them once or twice. But they were getting results, and I thought… maybe they could succeed where we had failed."

Emma's stomach twisted as she realized the full extent of his involvement. Thorne hadn't just turned a blind eye; he'd actively encouraged the Spectator's actions. She felt the weight of her disillusionment settle over her like a shroud. This man, the one she'd trusted above all others, had been complicit in a campaign of terror.

"So where does this end, Thorne?" she asked, her voice barely above a whisper. "How far does this network go?"

His expression softened, a glimmer of sorrow appearing in his eyes. "It goes farther than you'd think. And if you continue down this path, Emma, it'll eat you alive. Walk away. Don't let it consume you like it did me."

Emma shook her head, backing away as she held his gaze. "I can't do that. I won't let it keep happening."

Thorne watched her, his face shadowed in the early dawn light. "Then you're on your own, Emma. No one else in this department will back you up. Remember that."

Without another word, he turned and walked away, leaving her standing alone with the weight of her discovery. As he disappeared into the darkness, Emma knew she couldn't unsee the truth. The fight she faced was bigger than she'd imagined, and the path ahead would be perilous. But she also knew, deep in her heart, that she couldn't walk away. Not now. Not ever.

Chapter 33: A Final Confrontation

Emma stood in the dimly lit corridor of the precinct, the weight of her discovery bearing down on her shoulders like an invisible force. She'd spent the entire night piecing together the final threads of evidence, and every step had led her back to the man she once trusted beyond question—Inspector Thorne. The realization had left her shaken to her core, but the time for denial was over. She couldn't allow her loyalty or her emotions to compromise the truth, no matter how bitter the truth was.

She found Thorne in his office, his back turned as he stared out the window. The city lights cast a faint glow, illuminating his silhouette with an eerie calm. Emma's footsteps echoed through the room as she entered, and Thorne turned slowly, his expression unreadable. He didn't look surprised to see her. If anything, he looked resigned.

"Emma," he greeted her quietly. "I had a feeling you'd be here."

"I don't think you know why I'm here, Thorne." Her voice was steady, but the tension underneath was unmistakable. "I've been digging through the Spectator's victims, looking into every case you oversaw that somehow fell through the cracks. The connections, the favors—every piece of the puzzle led back to you."

Thorne sighed and looked down, almost as if he'd been expecting this moment all along. "I suppose it was only a matter of time before you found out," he said softly. "You're one of the best detectives I've ever known. I never doubted that you'd put the pieces together eventually."

The anger in Emma's chest flared. "So that's it? You're not even going to deny it?" She took a step closer, her voice trembling with both anger and hurt. "You protected them. You let murderers and criminals walk free. And for what? Some twisted idea that the Spectator's form of justice was better than the law?"

Thorne's gaze hardened. "Don't act like it's that simple, Emma. You know as well as I do how broken this system is. We've both seen how many times it fails the victims, how many criminals slip through the cracks because of politics, influence, or money." His voice grew more intense, a mix of anger and frustration. "I did what I had to, Emma. I thought that if I couldn't deliver justice within the system, then maybe I could find a way outside of it."

Emma shook her head, her heart sinking with each word he spoke. "You betrayed everything we stand for, Thorne. You betrayed me." She clenched her fists, fighting the urge to turn away. "You were supposed to be the one person I could trust."

He looked away, and for a moment, Emma thought she saw a flicker of regret cross his face. "I didn't want you to find out like this. I didn't want you involved in any of this. But I can't change what I've done, Emma. I believed… I still believe that the Spectator's actions, though brutal, served a purpose."

She took a deep breath, her mind racing. "People are dead, Thorne. Innocent people were caught in the crossfire. The Spectator wasn't a hero. They were a killer, and you enabled them."

Thorne's jaw tightened, and he looked at her with a mixture of desperation and defiance. "Do you think I haven't wrestled with that every day? Do you think I don't know the consequences of what I've done?" He clenched his fists. "But sometimes the price of real justice is too high for the system to pay. Someone had to do something."

Emma felt a surge of sadness as she realized that Thorne's moral compass, the one that had guided her own path, was shattered. "The ends don't justify the means, Thorne. You taught me that. Or was that just another lie?"

For a moment, neither of them spoke. The silence was thick with tension, and Emma's mind raced with memories of the cases they had worked on together, the late nights, the moments when she had leaned on his guidance and trusted him without question. She wondered how long he had been hiding this part of himself, how many lies had been told under the guise of mentorship.

"I didn't want you to see this side of me," Thorne admitted, his voice softer. "I wanted to keep you away from this darkness. But it's too late now. I see that. You're right to be angry, and you have every right to feel betrayed."

Emma's heart twisted as she took a step back, knowing what she had to do. "I didn't come here just for answers, Thorne. I came here because… I can't let this go. You know that."

He nodded slowly, resignation settling over him like a weight he could no longer bear. "I know, Emma. I knew this day would come, eventually." He took a deep breath, his voice calm but tinged with sadness. "But I want you to know that, despite everything, I am proud of you. You've become everything I hoped you would—a true seeker of justice."

She felt the sting of tears prickling at her eyes, but she forced them back. "Don't try to make this right, Thorne. Nothing about this is right."

"I'm not asking for forgiveness," he replied, his gaze steady. "I'm asking you to remember why we started this work in the first place. Even if my methods were flawed, I wanted to make this city a safer place."

Emma looked at him, trying to reconcile the man she'd respected with the man who now stood before her, admitting to crimes she could barely comprehend. "And where does that leave us now?"

Thorne's shoulders slumped, and he seemed to age before her eyes. "That's up to you, Emma. You're holding the cards now. If you turn me in, the network will crumble, and everything we've worked for... it will be exposed. But the city will be safer."

Emma knew that turning him in would mean exposing the entire network of corruption within the department. The fallout would be immense, and the city's trust in law enforcement would be shattered. But there was no other option. She couldn't let Thorne's actions, or the Spectator's, go unpunished. Justice had to mean something, even if it came at a cost.

Without another word, she reached for her phone and dialed Internal Affairs. She felt Thorne's gaze on her, heavy and unyielding, but she couldn't look at him. The betrayal was too raw, too close. As the call connected, she gave them her location, her voice steady as she reported the truth she'd uncovered.

Thorne stood silent, his expression resigned as he listened to her words. When she ended the call, he gave her a faint nod, a gesture that held a strange mix of pride and sorrow. "You did the right thing, Emma. Even if it hurts."

She didn't respond, the weight of her decision settling heavily on her shoulders. As the minutes passed, the sound of approaching footsteps echoed down the hallway, and a team of officers entered the room. They approached Thorne cautiously, cuffing him and reading him his rights. He didn't resist, his gaze locked on Emma's as they led him away.

When he was gone, Emma stood alone in the empty office, the silence around her echoing with the finality of what she'd done. The trust she'd placed in Thorne, the faith she'd had in the system—they were both shattered, but a new resolve began to build within her. She knew the fight ahead would be difficult, that the road to rebuilding trust would be long and uncertain. But she was ready to face it.

As she turned to leave, she paused at the door, looking back at the empty room one last time. The man she'd once looked up to was gone, replaced by the harsh truth she'd uncovered. But she knew she couldn't let it break her. She'd carry the weight of this betrayal, and she'd continue her work, no matter the cost. Because justice was worth fighting for, even in the face of those who'd betrayed it.

Chapter 34: The Unbreakable Oath

Emma sat in her car, staring blankly at the dimming skyline of the city she had fought to protect for so long. The weight of the past few months seemed to settle on her chest, making it difficult to breathe. The case had taken everything from her—her trust, her certainty, her peace of mind—and yet, it was far from over. The investigation into the Spectator, the web of corruption within the force, and the betrayal by the man she had once considered a mentor had all brought her to this moment of quiet reflection.

She didn't know how long she had been parked there, just looking out at the city that had both failed and shaped her. A soft knock on her window startled her, and she glanced over to see Detective Harris standing outside. She rolled down the window, forcing a tight smile. "You're still here?"

Harris didn't smile back. His eyes were tired, and there was a sorrow to his expression that she hadn't seen before. He had been with her throughout the investigation, but even he couldn't fully understand the toll it had taken on her. They had lost so much, and the cost of it all wasn't something that could easily be quantified.

"We're done, Emma," Harris said quietly. "The files are closed. Thorne's in custody. The Spectator's network is shattered. It's over."

Emma didn't respond immediately. Instead, she looked at the darkening skyline again. The city had been a battlefield for so long, and she had fought with everything she had to uncover the truth. Yet even now, with the case concluded and the perpetrators apprehended, she couldn't shake the feeling that the shadows of corruption would never truly be gone.

"Is it really over?" she asked, her voice soft, almost to herself.

Harris hesitated. "I think so. But I know you. I know you're not done. Not really."

She turned her gaze back to him, her eyes sharp. He wasn't wrong. There was no way she could let go of this. She had made a promise to herself, one that she hadn't even fully realized until now. A promise to never stop fighting. A vow to never let the city fall back into the hands of those who had used their power for personal gain.

"I have to be," Emma said finally. "I have to keep fighting. Even if it costs me everything."

Harris nodded, his expression unreadable. "I get it. You've always been driven by this... the need to protect people. But, Emma, sometimes you have to let go. You can't carry the weight of the world on your shoulders."

She shook her head, her jaw set. "I can't let go. Not when I know how deep the corruption runs. It's not just about one person, or even one case. It's about a system that's broken, that's been broken for years. And if I walk away now, nothing changes."

"You're not alone, Emma," Harris said. "You've got a team. You've got people who believe in you."

She looked at him, appreciating his words, but she couldn't shake the feeling that he didn't fully understand. He wasn't the one who had lost everything. He wasn't the one who had trusted the wrong people. He hadn't stood at the edge of a precipice, wondering if it was all worth it.

"I know," she said, her voice steady but tired. "But I have to do this on my own. I have to keep my integrity intact."

Harris watched her for a moment, then gave a slow nod. "Just remember, Emma, you don't have to do it alone. We're here. Don't forget that."

She gave him a brief, grateful smile before he turned and walked away, disappearing into the growing darkness of the night. Emma sat there for a long moment, the sounds of the city around her muffled in her mind. The case had ended, but the war within her was far from over.

The truth she had uncovered, the lies she had been forced to confront, and the betrayal she had suffered—it all weighed heavily on her, but she couldn't let it destroy her. The city was broken, yes, but she would be its protector. She would be the shield that stood between the corrupt and the innocent, no matter the cost.

Her phone buzzed in the silence, breaking her reverie. She glanced at the screen, recognizing the number immediately. It was Internal Affairs. She had expected this call, but the sense of finality still made her heart race. She took a deep breath before answering.

"Emma," the voice on the other end greeted her. "The files on Thorne and the Spectator are moving forward. The investigation is over, but there's more we need to discuss. We'll be in touch."

Emma didn't say anything for a moment, just absorbing the weight of the words. The case was closed, but the repercussions would continue to ripple through the department and the city for years to come. She had no illusions about what it meant. This wasn't just the end of an investigation—it was the beginning of a new chapter, one where the work was never truly finished. One where the fight for justice never ended.

She ended the call and leaned back in her seat, her hands gripping the steering wheel. She had been a detective for years, but now the mantle of responsibility felt different. Heavier. The truth she had uncovered had left her with scars, emotional and professional, but they were hers to carry. She had made a promise to herself that she wouldn't turn away from the darkness, no matter how much it threatened to swallow her.

She couldn't let the city fall back into the hands of those who had exploited it for so long. No matter how many times it tried to break her, she would keep fighting. Emma had learned the hard way that the path to justice was never easy, and the system would never change unless people like her stood up to it. She would be that person.

The engine of the car roared to life, and Emma pulled away from the curb. She didn't look back. The city was waiting, and there was still work to be done.

As she drove through the streets, the city lights flickering around her, Emma made a silent vow. She would never again let her guard down. She would never stop fighting for the truth, no matter where it led her. She would continue to seek justice, even when it seemed impossible. The shadows might never fully dissipate, but as long as she was here, she would stand as a beacon against them.

An unshakable commitment to justice. An unbreakable oath to serve. And a promise to never stop.

Did you love *The Watcher's Silent Crusade : A Police Procedurals & Crime Thriller*? Then you should read *The Echoing Room A Psychological Thriller*[1] by Kraken!

[2]

In the fog-shrouded town of Millbrook, Dr. Evelyn Caldwell's meticulously controlled life is shattered when a new patient's haunting words—"The carousel never stops spinning"—set off a cascade of repressed memories. As Evelyn delves into the dark secrets of her past, she uncovers chilling parallels between her life and the mysterious disappearance of her patient, Lila Matthews. With a series of grisly murders tied to her own childhood, Evelyn must confront a sinister cult, The Circle, and its charismatic leader, Gabriel Stone. As the lines between healer and victim blur, Evelyn races against time to unravel a web of generational trauma and find the strength to break the cycle of abuse that has haunted her family for decades. "The Echoing Room " is a thrilling psychological thriller in which every turn reveals a deeper layer of darkness and every shadow hides a new truth.

---

1. https://books2read.com/u/mq5k58
2. https://books2read.com/u/mq5k58

Also by Marcelo Palacios

El Club de los Pecados Un Thriller Psicológico
La Habitación Resonante Un Thriller Psicológico
Mentiras en Código Un Thriller Político
The Political Lies A Political Thriller
Sin's Fraternity A Psychological Thriller
El Cuarto de los Ecos Un Thriller Psicologico lleno de Suspenso
The Room of Echoes A Psychological Thriller Full of Suspense
El Espejo Perturbador Un Thriller Psicologico
The Disturbing Mirror A Psychological Thriller
Luces Apagadas en la Ciudad Brillante Un Thriller Psicológico, Crimen y Policial
Lights Out in the Shining City A Psychological, Crime and Police Thriller
Under the Cloak of Horror A Criminal Psychological Thriller full of Abuse, Corruption, Mystery, Suspense and Adventure
The Housemaid's Shadow A Psychological Thriller
Unraveling Marriage, Unraveling Divorce A Domestic Thriller
Mindstorm Protocol Expansion : A Post-Apocalyptic, Dystopian and Technological Thriller Science Fiction Novel
The Power of Invisible Chains : A Conspiracy, Crime & Political Thriller
The Watcher's Silent Crusade : A Police Procedurals & Crime Thriller
Very Bad Momentum : A Short Story

Milton Keynes UK
Ingram Content Group UK Ltd.
UKHW042002291124
451915UK00004B/380